A
LEGACY
OF
CHAINS
AND OTHER STORIES

A LEGACY OF CHAINS

AND OTHER STORIES

PHILIP
KRASKE

encompass
EDITIONS

Published by Encompass Editions, Kingston, Ontario, Canada.
No part of this book may be reproduced, copied or used in any form or manner
whatsoever without written permission, except for the purposes of brief
quotations in reviews and critical articles. For reader comments,
orders, press and media inquiries:
www.encompasseditions.com
or
www.philipkraske.com

FIRST EDITION 2021
ISBN 978-1-927664-17-9
Cataloguing in Publication
Program (CIP) information available from
Library and Archives Canada
at www.collectionscanada.gc.ca

Cover Design by Ismael Medina
ismael@virgen-extra.com

encompass
E D I T I O N S

To Carlos and Mara

CONTENTS

And when Jesus was come near,
he beheld the city, and wept over it.
– Luke 19:41

A LEGACY OF CHAINS

A NIGHT IN SEPTEMBER, and there were five of us scattered around the backyard patio: two couples and our host Ram, at that moment between marriages. His barbecued steaks had been tender, his wine tangy, and his salad crunchy between the molars. The tomatoes had traveled but twenty meters in their lives from his garden to his table. The dinner was itself an act of defiance, the area being on "voluntary lockdown" due to increasing terrorist activity in the area. A week earlier, not three blocks away, the assistant secretary of defense had been blown sky-high with his wife and two children. Drone attacks – hand-sized drones with three or four powerful firecrackers wired together (instructions available on the Internet), flown in through open government doors and windows and detonated – had become so commonplace that radio-jammers to thwart them shredded cell-phone coverage. A dark time – the kind of darkness history is cut from.

Which was why Ram – what else could you call a fellow named Ramón Ramirez? – had called up "the gang" and invited us over:

"And not a word about politics until the steaks are eaten and the dishes cleared away. I am not kidding. Until I have a a full stomach and a double whiskey in my hand, we talk about kids, redecorating the house, and investment op's in Singapore. I want to hear all the latest about Cindy's recovery from spinal injury and Wanda's cookbook-contract dispute. Period."

A tall order. All day the news bulletins had peppered the airwaves: the California, Oregon, and Washington legislatures, having declared independence together, were mulling the president's ultimatum to "stand down" – why does everyone speak in military terms in this country? – or be left to the tender mercies of the Pentagon.

A long swath of states running up the center of the country from Texas to the Canadian border, fed up with Washington for a variety of reasons, were conferring on taking the same steps; wags suggested calling it The Flyover Republic. The old Dixie states were not far behind; many natives were actively urging "Northerners" to leave.

And everywhere huge fights were breaking out in high schools and colleges – sometimes in offices. Well-founded rumor had it that the Pentagon didn't know which way their people in uniform were going to shoot if it came to a showdown between Washington and breakaway states. A Marine general was fired after declaring that he would not order his troops to turn their weapons on fellow Americans.

The mainstream media outlets, seeing their revenues in jeopardy, were pulling hard in the direction of unity, and rolled out one platitudinous promo after another: *What unites us is far greater than our differences. It's precisely our diversity that makes us strong. Our two hundred-plus years of democratic fair play – listening to the other person and really trying to see his or her or its point of view – have always been the real key to our success as a nation.* They accused the Chinese of financing the separatists and the Russians of backing them with logistics and hacking. The alternative media, however, reported that the real power behind the separatists was two Big Tech billionaires, and the evidence for this was by no means flimsy. As the miasma of reportage swarmed higher and stronger, so did anxiety and anger.

Obeying Ram's order was easier than I'd expected; we'd all had enough of politics. We did indeed review the progress of offspring, careers, markets, and Cindy's rehabilitation: a decade after a fall had damaged her spinal cord, she was now walking – with the use of a cane when tired – her improvement the fruit of daily two-hour rehabilitation exercises and expensive growth-hormone injections that the insurance companies declared "too experimental" and would not pay for. Husband Paul and she had been on a shoestring budget for years, but content nonetheless.

And as long as I'm on the subject, let me fill out the cast. My old friend Paul Klippen was a State

Department veteran of several posts, currently at Foggy Bottom itself. Ram was a partner in and top programmer of a software company, a job that absorbed him about sixty hours a week, to his ex-wives' chagrin. My wife Wanda was a part-time cookbook writer and executive in the DoT: that's the Department of Transportation. In Washington one gets so damnably inured to abbreviations and acronyms that they bounce off the tongue as easily as verbs. The habit drives to distraction my brother and sister in London.

Which brings me to your narrator: Max Venable, fiftyish professor of Caribbean studies at Georgetown University. I was an active MI6 agent until – as I relate in greater detail in *11/9 and the Terrorist Who Loved Bonsai Trees* – I was rendered inactive during a life-changing encounter with Mexican drug thugs, this arranged by the CIA cousins: they were upset when I refused to hand over my agents for them to burn. I'm afraid loyalty has always been a bit of a thing with me.

Which point – loyalty – brings me to our story, of which Paul Klippen is the star.

Among the many reasons I admire Paul is that, though he had worked in the State Department since his late twenties, he had always considered himself a public servant and representative of his people. There was always something very Kansas City about Paul: his love of jazz, basketball and hard work. His sheer decency probably made him a poor fit for the sleaziness of international relations, which he had stepped into for the adventure and sheer intellectual challenge of it all. His twenty-something years of foreign and domestic postings and the occasional sleaziness therein had produced a refreshingly mature and philosophical mind.

So when after-dinner drinks had been poured and a few sweaters donned against the chilly air, and we began turning over the present political mess, graduating to the question of when it had started – *When did people begin to turn against their government?* – it was Paul who provided the real answer.

Cindy and Ram said it Donald Trump and his antics that had split the nation, leading to huge protests and the rise of violent right-wing groups, infused as whites often are with a sense of their racial superiority.

Wanda, our local radical who wanted to make all urban public transportation free, said it was the military-security complex that had turned the government into a quasi-dictatorship.

I opined that the problem went back further, to Ronald Reagan's dangerous dictum that "government isn't the answer; it's the problem." "After Reagan," I thundered, "you had to be a foolish politician indeed not to 'run against Washington!'"

Which left Paul, who at the head of Ram's picnic table sat on the back of the chair with his feet on its seat, hunched over the iced Cointreau in his hands. He had an open, well-cut face and wore roundish glasses, always marvelously clean. "Viet-nam," he said, and just that word on the night air had a chilling sound to it: so many images of ban-daged G.I.s., raging hippy protesters, and hard-edged White House men in cropped hair. All of us there were still in nappies when it ended, but Vietnam, we knew, was not just a country.

"Vietnam," he repeated with a dazed shake of his head. "Who'd have thought America would turn itself inside-out over a long string of swamp and mountain on the other side of the world? Be-fore the war, government – even bureaucrats like my uncles who worked in the forests and regulated the food industry – was respected. After Vietnam, people looked on government with suspicion and bitterness."

I realized what Paul was thinking of. "And it ran both ways, didn't it, old fruit? After Vietnam, the fellows in high places had no patience with the *hoi polloi* and its yammering."

Paul looked at me a long time over his drink. "Or its lives," he added.

"Why don't you tell them, old man?" I said. "Bloody good story, and it was never an official se-cret; *officially* it never happened."

"What, what?" Wanda chirped alertly. "Some-thing dirty, Paul?"

Ram had also dictated that all cell phones must be turned off for the evening, though he would keep his on just in case something important hap-pened. Now his phone squealed and he read the news flash on his screen. "Shit. The director of OMB just had his car blown up."

That's the Office of Management and Budget.

"The police are investigating the explosion. They're telling everyone to stay inside until midnight. They're on to suspects."

"That sounds ominous," said Cindy. "It's like after the Boston Marathon Massacre."

Silence.

"Which means it's a perfect moment for a story, Paul," said Wanda, to an gargle of chuckling.

"It's pretty involved."

"The longer and more involved the better, seems to me. For the moment, we're on curfew."

Cindy snatched Paul's glass and with her oddly mechanical gait, crossed the patio to the drinks table. "I never get to hear any of the dirt, either," she complained over her shoulder. "Eighteen years of marriage, and all I get are a few smiles and frowns when I ask how the day went."

"I fend off invasions of the yellow hordes and prevent nuclear war, Cin," Paul retorted. "It's not pretty."

"Do you know this story, you rat?" Wanda asked.

"Actually had a small role in it, old love."

"I don't care. You're still a rat."

Cindy handed Paul his glass, and he looked at it for a long moment. "Vietnam – my goodness. Whatever we got after that, we deserved."

****

"This was before my time as a big shot in Washington," Paul began, "when the secretary of state resigned and things were in flux for a while. I muscled my way into a vacancy in Embassy Madrid. They could hardly refuse: I'd had three hardship postings in a row: Cameroon, Morocco, and Ecuador. It was fantastic: I speak Spanish, and Cindy and I have always loved Europe."

"Especially the wine," Cindy added, raising her glass.

"I was in post for about nine months when one morning at about five a.m. my phone rang and someone on the embassy night staff told me that a boatload of American refugees had washed up on the southern shore of Spain, having crossed the Straits of Gibraltar from Morocco. Very strange news: the ones who wash up on Spanish shores from Morocco tend to be Congolese, Nigerians, Libyans, Liberians – not folks from Peoria.

"He patched me through to a Red Cross rep down on the coast, in the small city of Tarifa. Are we talking about kids out joyriding from Gibraltar? I asked her.

"By no means, came the answer. They were all men in their seventies.

"Have you looked at their passports, their wallets, a drivers license?

"No, they have no identification whatsoever. Not so much as a cell phone.

"Are any or all of them injured or sick?

"No. They are in good condition, and in excellent spirits. *Sobradamente contentos,* she said: extremely happy. But they would have nothing to do with the Red Cross and demanded to speak to a US. Embassy representative.

"Where can I find them?

"On the dock at Tarifa."

Paul sighed. "So: shower, shave, suit, tie, leather shoes. Half of diplomacy is looking the part, you know. I grabbed the first high-speed-train out for the south coast. I hoped to sleep a little, but you can't help but watch the seas of olive trees and white-washed villages and tenth-century castles on the mountaintops; in Spain you are hard put to find a boring view.

"In Malaga I rented a car, and still had no idea what to expect. Best guess? There's an American naval base up the coast about eighty miles or so: maybe these were old ship buddies who'd been having a reunion on a boat, which had become disabled.

"It took me an hour to reach the city of Tarifa, which is on the southernmost point of Spain, looking directly across the Straits at the mountains of Morocco. It divides the Mediterranean from the Atlantic. Classic Spanish: white-washed and packed together amidst alleyways even more narrow than normal villages. It's the best defense against the *Levante* wind, which three or four days a week roars westwards through the straits, compressed by the European and African continents.

Just to walk across the street, from the last of the town to the port, nearly blew my jacket off me. The port is built with a fifty-foot wall on the east side just to keep the wind off the Coast Guard ships towing boatloads of illegal immigrants in off the Mediterranean: Spain's version of the Rio Grande, you know.

"And just like they'd told me, there were the men: nine of them, thin, gray, old enough to be my father, four of them napping on the stone ledge along the wall, having rolled up their Red Cross blankets and used them for pillows. That immediately struck me: they could sleep on hard rock. Others were eating sandwiches and sipping juice from small cartons, talking to the two Guardias Civiles – Spain's national police force. They were evidently talking about bullfighting: one of the Guardias was demonstrating how the matador had to keep his back straight when the bull ran through the cape. Now they all laughed about something. Seemed to be a pretty amiable crew.

"At the entrance to the port – just inside the wall in order to be out of the wind – I talked to the Guardia Civil captain and the rather nervous Red Cross lady in her red safety vest, the one I'd talked to before. They told me little that I hadn't heard before, except for two odd things. One or two of the men didn't even speak English. When the Red Cross lady and the one Guardia Civil who spoke some English talked to the men, one man was translating the conversation to someone behind him who obviously spoke no English – translating in *Chinese*. Also, an hour earlier they had asked about political-refugee status."

"Just a sec', Paul," Ram interrupted. "Another bulletin: the police are pursuing three suspects in the Arlington area. Residents are ordered – yes, ordered – to stay indoors."

"I always thought the people in Arlington were crooks," joked Cindy.

"Let's forget the world outside, okay?" said Wanda. "Go on, Paul."

"Well, I pushed my hair back into place and put on my best State Department face and walked down the port to the men. Instantly a cheer went up, and the sleeping men awoke and jumped down from the ledge. A few started towards me, but were called back – in Chinese, but not quite – by the tallest of them, a distinguished-looking fellow: bald, light mustache and goatee, and thin like all of them. They seemed to be healthy, just sort-of banged-up looking. It was as if they'd been dropped in a barrel, rolled around, and then shaken out. At his call, they recoiled, and the group formed behind this man, clearly their leader.

"I told them who I was and flashed my State i.d.. The tall man stepped forward and shook my hand.

"'John Milner, I'm a doctor.'

"'And where are you from, Dr. Milner?'

"'*From?*' Milner chuckled, and so did the men, as if this were some kind of inside joke. I noticed now that their teeth were awful: not one was without a few blank spaces.

"'Well now, *from*, if we're going to talk *from*. I'm *from* Hudson, Wisconsin.' He half-turned to the men and said something – not in Chinese, but for the life of me I could not place it – and the men roared with laughter. 'Todd over there is from Milwaukee. And let's see...we've got one from Philadelphia, one from West Virginia, the Captain over there is from Texas, ah, two Californians, one Iowan and...McAnder, where you from? Never asked.'

"'Little ol' Preston, Georgia,' said the only black man of the group.

"'So as far as *from* goes, that's where we're *from*,' said Milner. He had a handsome face for a man in his seventies. It was marred only by a smile that lifted only one side of his face and showed his molars – one missing – which gave him the look of a riverboat gambler with an ace up his sleeve. 'Though where we've come from *today* is a fruit freighter that slowed down early this morning as it was nearing the Straits of Gibraltar. They lowered a ladder for us and a rubber raft. Guy on the bridge radioed in to the Coast Guard that a boatload of refugees was out there floating around. We were hoping to make the Rock of Gibraltar, but that damn wind kept blowing us west, and they came and got us just a few miles out from here. So that's where we're from.' The grin opened again, as if there were a joke in all this.

"Which I didn't get, and I was starting to get impatient. 'A strange story, Doctor. And what can the State Department do for you today?'

"'We are political refugees. We are fleeing political persecution.'

"'So they've told me – though I think you needn't fear political persecution from Uncle Sam. It's something we kind of pride ourselves on.'

"'On the face of things, yes, on the face of things. But the moment you hear our story, the persecution begins.'

"The black man bubbled a translation to some others, and now the men's faces were tight.

"I waited. 'Well, Doctor, as the saying goes, Let's get this party started.'

"Milner was about to reply when from behind him came a joyful shout:

"'We're American P.O.W.s from V'etnam!'

"'Escaped!' added another.

"The men cheered again. Milner gazed at me with his lopsided grin.

"Well, it was too amazing not to be true. After a bit of stammering, I pulled out my cell phone and looked up the Vietnam War Memorial. Its web page has a search engine, and in a few seconds I found Captain John S. Milner, surgeon, presumed dead in 1971 in a helicopter crash. Then I looked up McAnder, and there it was: first name Mark, corporal, gone missing in Quang Tri in 1968, presumed dead."

"A typical day in the life of an American diplomat," Paul's wife Cindy assured us.

"I'll drink to that," Paul said, and he did. "Well! This was either the world's most elaborate practical joke, or the world's biggest surprise. I ought to put in here that the Vietnam War had ended in 1973; this was happening in 2010."

"Thirty-seven years," said Ram from the hammock. "And they'd all been taken prisoner for years before that, probably."

"Two of them seven years before the war ended, it would turn out." Paul took a breath. "Well, what to do? I couldn't keep them on the port, and both the Guardia Civil captain and the Red Cross had said that they were expecting two boatloads of African refugees within the hour. They wanted the men taken off their hands. I thought fast.

"'All right, gents,' I told them. 'First of all, congrats on your escape; I'd love to hear all about it. Here's what we'll do. There's a big American naval base up the Atlantic coast here – hour's drive away. I'll call them up and they can send some kind of bus or mini-van. Can all of you travel all right? No broken bones?'

"'No,' said Milner, 'that won't –'

"'They must have *some* kind of vehicle big enough. I can take three guys in my –'

"'Klippen, would you shut up?' snapped Milner. 'You don't get this at all. We were *abandoned* in V'etnam. The Pentagon has always flatly denied that any P.O.W.s were left behind. What – you

22

think they're going to be happy to see us back? We're the biggest embarrassment since Watergate. We got left behind and a lot of other poor devils did too. It's the *State Department* that has to handle this, and keep the Pentagon away from us until this is all cleared up.'

"'Dr. Milner, please: I'm sure that isn't –'

"'Listen, the captain ordered us off that ship because the U.S. Navy is looking for us. Somehow they have a lead on where we are. They were sending him messages about terrorists aboard his ship. They wanted to board and search it. The man didn't want to take chances, and I can't blame him. You take us to that naval base and they might well helicopter us out into the Atlantic and toss us to the sharks.'

"I looked at the other men, and it was clear from their grim faces that they thought the same thing." Paul looked up into the night sky. "And now, from way, way, way back, the vaguest memory winged me: there *had* been some kind of controversy after the war that the Vietnamese hadn't returned all American P.O.W.s."

"There was a Sylvester Stallone *Rambo* movie about it," said Ram, and Cindy nodded.

"I saw it, dear." A grin. "He has a body that just won't quit."

Paul smiled. "Well, I realized that I didn't have any idea what my move was. So I said to Milner, 'All right, Doctor, you and the men know more about the issue than I do. What would you like me to do?'

"'Two options, Klippen: one, you talk to the local officials and certify that we're Americans and turn us over to the Red Cross and the Spanish government. We'll ask for status as political refugees, but God only knows what that will get us. *Or,* much better, you handle this on your own. Maybe you can find us a place to stay and scout the terrain a little for us. I can pay for accommodations.'

"What Milner didn't know was that the Red Cross and the government were already overwhelmed with refugees. It was early October, and the last wave of illegals was making the crossing before the weather got too bad.

"I must have thought this over too long, because he went on: 'Well, whatever you do, do it right now. If the Navy's sent out someone to search that ship and found we're not there, it's hard to say if they'll believe the captain's denials – not to mention the crew's, because they know all about us as well. And they'll come looking for us. But if they haven't boarded, then we've got some breathing room. In fact' – he handed me a slip of paper with *Albert Boyd III* written on it along with a long satellite phone number – 'one smart thing to do would be to call the ship's captain and ask if they've searched the ship.'"

My wife Wanda now interjected with her famous, "Now just hold on a ding-dong minute here." When I hear the *ding-dong minute,* I know that protestations of outrage are imminent. "Obama was president. You could have gone straight to Washington with the problem. He would have called off the dogs and welcomed them home with medals on their chests. No way. No way, no way, no way."

Wanda always had a rather idealistic image of Obama.

Paul hesitated and, ever the diplomat, said, "Well, Wanda, let me tell you the story, and you can judge for yourself. Me, I don't think the matter ever got to his desk."

He got down from the chair, whose back biting into his behind must have been smarting by now. He sat normally at the head of the picnic table, drink in front of him between his well-shaped hands.

"I made the first decision: the immediate thing to do was eliminate as many traces of the men as I could: if the Navy wasn't on to the men today, it would be tomorrow.

"So I called together a quick huddle of the Guardias Civiles and the Red Cross lady and put the fear of God in them: 'I'm afraid I have bad news. I'm just going to lay it down straight, since you're just here doing your jobs and you don't deserve this.' A breath. 'These men are top-secret Cold War prisoners who've escaped from the base up the coast; they were in transit. Nobody was ever supposed to lay eyes on them, and the CIA will soon come calling for anyone who has. If you don't want trouble, erase all this: from your phones, your reports, your agendas – everything. Don't let anyone trace you to these men *or* their arrival.'

"The Red Cross rep's hand had fluttered up to her mouth. The men were murmuring obscenities: *'Me cago en dios...la ostia puta.'*

"I turned to the Guardia Civil captain. 'I'll need some kind of van to take the men away in. And you'll need to bury any trace of the men with the Coast Guard, understand?'

"'Yes, no problem. I'll do it right now.'

"Well, that sent everyone scurrying. Meanwhile, I called a Spanish friend who had a villa down the coast some fifteen miles. Remember when we were there, Cindy?"

"Yeah. What a place! Three hundred feet over the ocean, and only a quarter mile back from the shore. That's how the better half lives."

"Alvaro came from old money. He generally used the place for his orgies."

"He *was* a greasy little skunk. He offered to show his sexual technique one morning when you were down in the town market."

"You fended him off, I hope?"

"I did my best, dear."

"Be that as it may," Paul went on when the laughter had subsided. "The Guardia Civil captain called his uncle and said I could rent his mini-van – the only large vehicle available on the spur of the moment. A lot of men would have to sit on the floor, which would be damn uncomfortable, but there was haste to be made. While we were waiting for it to arrive, I called the captain of the *Albert Boyd III*. I talked to him as if I were the Red Cross and said that the men had insisted I let him know they had landed safely and wanted to thank him one last time – and by the way, did the U.S. Navy board you? He said no. They had wanted him to pull into the naval base at Rota for them to search the ship, but he had given them hell about how that would mess up his schedule and cost him money, and they finally backed down. When I called, he had already passed by their base and was steaming for Newark, about five days ahead.

"So: either the Navy wasn't sure they were on board or they were and didn't have ships available to interdict. That was my reading of them. The base is basically just a refueling place for their ships going into and out of the Med." Paul shook his head. "Was I ever wrong about that one. Oh, I got a lot of things wrong in this case, folks."

"You did the best anyone could, old man," I put in.

Paul shrugged. "I figured that they couldn't be sure about where the men were, so I at least had a few hours in which to put some kind of temporary bandage on the problem." He drank. "To be honest, I wasn't all that sure about Milner's theory of how the men would be received. Americans don't have a terribly long historical memory to start with, and nine men returning from Vietnam

– hell, it seemed to me that one way or another, the issue could be finessed."

"*Obama* could have finessed it," Wanda said. "He could've finessed anything."

"But just to be on the safe side, I turned off my cell phone and left it in my rental car. Then I drove the men up the Atlantic coast to a town called Zahara de los Atunes. We passed through town and then rose up through street after street of chic white villas with window-walls looking out over the Atlantic. It's called the German Barrio because apparently ex-Nazis were allowed to retire there in style after World War Two. Nowadays you find the Russian mafia. Matilda, Alvaro's maid, flagged me down where she was standing in front of a gate in the high wall around the place. She handed me the keys and was surprised to see, rather than twentyish nymphs, nine old men who tumbled out of the van and through the gate. She had provisionally stocked the place with food and condoms. The men were grateful for the former and tickled by the latter.

"After a quick lunch, the men tumbled off to the bedrooms and sofa to sleep off the busy night – except Milner. He stripped and threw himself into what must have been a very cold swimming pool."

"One of those infinity pools," Cindy interjected. "You could stand in it with your arms on the pool deck sipping your margarita, and the view must have been fifty miles out into the Atlantic. You could watch the ships coming out of the Straits and turning north or south."

"One tough old guy, that Milner," Paul went on. "I immediately admired him. I made coffee, and he filled me in on their escape from Vietnam.

"He had finished his pre-med studies at the University of Wisconsin in the mid-Sixties when he enlisted in the Army on the promise that he could work in military hospitals. He was an orphan and from a young age had been brought up by his aunt and uncle, the uncle a cattle doctor who attended sick cows, pigs and horses all over western Wisconsin. At ten Milner was helping his uncle operate on the animals, and by fifteen he was operating himself under the direction of his uncle. They worked in barns, on bare floors strewn with whatever clean hay they could find. His uncle's only complaint was that he could never work on his patient on an operating table: long stretches of kneeling on hard floors had ruined his knees. Milner was a veteran surgeon even before he'd finished high school.

"Milner began working in Saigon hospitals in 1968, at the height of the war. At first he did three or four months of assisting surgeons, then began doing simple surgery, though mainly just the basic job of extracting bullets and shrapnel so that the real doctors could finish up. But after a year and amidst the rising crowds of wounded, he was put to work like any other surgeon, and only rarely had to call in a pro. When his term was up, he re-enlisted and continued without a hitch.

"'And it was the East – the Orient!' he exclaimed to me over his coffee mug. 'All green mountains and people with those broad coolie hats, just like in encyclopedia pictures. Demure girls with glowing smiles. Happy market ladies with three teeth left in their mouths. I was in love with it. I paid a guy to teach me the language and I soaked it up like a sponge. If it hadn't been for the poor shot-up bastards being brought to me every day at the hospital, I'd have considered it a paid vacation.'

"But he also wanted to see something of the war itself, and in 1971 got himself assigned to a medevac helicopter picking up the wounded out in the field. But one day, as his crew arrived, a battle re-erupted, the helicopter was hit, and North Vietnamese soldiers popped up on every side hardly a stone's-throw away.

"Milner was unhurt, had his arm-band that marked him as a doctor and his already-good Vietnamese. The wounded Americans were taken along. 'That was the policy,' Milner explained: 'take as many prisoners as possible. Didn't understand it at the time – who needed the extra mouths to feed and clothe? But the North was playing the long game: the more P.O.W.s they had, the more hostages they could bargain with in negotiations. Some died on the way? No problem. The thing was to have a nice long list of the missing.' He ran a hand over his small beard. 'Fools. They never figured the Nixon people wouldn't give a damn.'

"The prisoners got the whole P.O.W. treatment: starvation, torture, beatings. In that, Milner was lucky. His group ended up at a jungle base-camp, and there were a lot of Viet Cong wounded, so Milner told his captors he was willing to tend both Americans and Vietnamese. He was kept under tight surveillance, but his skill was obvious: after three years he had seen every possible wound, burn, break, and infection known to man. From there, he worked his way north, from camp to camp. Twice he witnessed the savagery of bombing raids. He watched a B-52 fly right over him, bombs falling, but the closest one was a dud, and the next struck some quarter-mile downrange; the ground shook and rolled under him for a full minute.

"Then he was in Hanoi: surgeon by day, prisoner by night. The Vietnamese didn't quite know what to do with him, and he moved between two or three hospitals for a time, always under guard. Then finally he was moved to a stone fortress in the center of the city; he would later learn that it was French-built for their colonial administration: The Citadel, it was called. There he had a room with bars on the window, and rather than a pallet to sleep on he had a hammock. His food improved; he had to cook his own on a little gas fire – chicken, vegetables, spicy fish sauce that nurses gave him, shyly grateful for having saved their brothers or cousins.

"He did nothing but work, sleep and continue to build his Vietnamese. After about two years, when the news came of the war ending, he had just finished operating on a general's optical nerve. Six months later, he asked the hospital director when he would be sent back to America. He'd heard about an exchange of prisoners. Should he continue to take on new cases?

"'Well, he didn't answer, and I figured they wanted to keep me on. Which was fine with me. I was doing every kind of surgery in the book, a lot of it by the seat of my pants; in the States, they would have thrown me in jail. But just about everything I did was successful. I was a real stickler for procedure and post-op care – learned that in Saigon. In the tropics, you have to be on top of post-op, or infection sets in fast. Any nurse who didn't change bandages on time, oh, I reduced her to tears, and if she did it twice she got a series of good hard slaps. No one complained. The opposite: when the other doctors saw my results, they bore down on procedure and post-op too, and pretty soon we had the best hospital in the country, north or south. All the top brass insisted on being treated there – and preferably by me. And that meant budget, prestige and privilege.

"'Things went on till finally one day – must've been a year or two on after the war, '74 or '75 – I pointed out to the hospital director that I didn't mind staying on in 'Nam, but they couldn't keep treating me like a prisoner *and* their best surgeon. I wasn't bucking to trouble the waters, just to square the situation with the U.S. and get on with my work. Even *then* I had two or three research projects under way.

"'Well, they hemmed and hawed for a few months; I knew perfectly well what the hold-up was. Now and then an American or Australian P.O.W. came into the hospital – shot-down pilots most of them. When I asked the director about it, they said that V'etnam was holding back some prisoners to be sure the U.S. didn't start bombing again. Could be. By then the North had re-invaded and taken the South – lazy bums, the South V'et-namese. It was a walkover. But for a long time people feared the Americans would come back: the anti-aircraft guns stayed where they were around The Citadel. But they never did. I was a bit sur-prised, to be honest, after the North won. But it seemed that Uncle Sam had had enough.

"'Then one night on the radio there was this long anti-American diatribe and someone read a letter from President Nixon to the V'etnamese prime minister, Pham Van Dong. Turned out Nix-on had promised in writing to pay war reparations – about 3.75 billion dollars, which was real money back when they signed in '73. The beef was that the Yankees weren't paying up. That's when I realized I was in for the long haul. The left-over P.O.W.s were being held as hostages.'"

"I don't believe that," blurted Wanda. "We signed a treaty and then didn't pay up? Forget it. This is America. We *abide by* our obligations."

"Yes and no, Wanda," Paul replied. "The treaty mentioned payments to North Vietnam, but not a specific number. During negotiations, a separate committee was formed to hash out the amount. The result was Nixon's letter to the Vietnamese premier."

"How much is that in today's money?" asked Cindy.

"On it," said Ram, tapping on his cell phone. "Okay...3.75 billion then is 21.88 billion today. That'd fund a couple of federal departments but good."

"And we didn't pay?" Wanda insisted.

"The North, I think, got suckered there," said Paul. "They hadn't insisted on the number being in the treaty. In fact, the Nixon letter was secret and didn't come to light until after Nixon had resigned." He drank. "Where was I?"

"Milner at the hospital, old fruit," I called from the drinks bar. "He's getting his status normalized."

"Okay. Milner got his answer from the director two months later when a very pretty new nurse was assigned to be his personal secretary. Thirty years later, he still laughed about it – with that odd sideways mouth of his:

"'Oh, they are a ham-fisted lot, the V'etnamese,' he told me, using the pronunciation that the men were accustomed to, skipping the I. 'Subtlety is just not their strong suit. They had assigned someone to be my wife – and to spy on me and make sure I didn't try to bolt.' He had no interest in women beyond the physical, so he did what was expected and married her. When children arrived, he was moved to a spacious apartment in the city, the government having figured that he was now rooted in Vietnam. He laughed at that too. 'Such stupidity: anyone with a brain could have seen that my root in Hanoi was my work. What future would I have had in the States? To start med school all over again? I could have taught Master's courses in surgery by then.'

"More and more cancer patients were arriving in Hanoi, and Milner realized that he was seeing the delayed effect of the massive bombing and chemical spraying that the country had withstood for a decade. He asked for literature on cancer treatment – the hospital would get him any medical journal in the world – and sought out country doctors for advice; he had watched with awe how they worked in jungle prison camps, curing with a few gathered grasses and root juices everything from snakebite to rheumatism. His fellow doctors in the hospital disdained them as quacks; Milner put them – his colleagues, I mean – to shame. By the mid-Nineties, his cancer department, on a shoestring budget, not a single computer, and with the absolute minimum of high-tech, rivaled any in the world for success rates against cancer.

"'Until the damn Americans came along and made dropping the national health system a requirement for V'etnam to enter the World Trade Organization. They were real bastards about it, and our funding went to hell. But there it was. They were determined to get their damn health-care chains into the country. Took us years to get back on track.'

"He began travelling to the Soviet Union and its satellites – always accompanied by two security men to be sure he didn't bolt – and was corresponding with a university hospital in Australia, though always with an intel person reading his messages. He received invitations to give presentations, but the Vietnamese didn't trust him and refused to let him go. Which always rankled: 'I could have spilled the beans about my being a prisoner in a dozen different ways. In Moscow I had a valid New Zealand passport and could have given my guards the slip. But those shits in the defense ministry never let me travel anywhere except to Russia and East Europe, and always under guard. Keeping the secret about their holding P.O.W.s was the priority, and that was that.'

"In the late 90s, he began to bring the left-over American prisoners into the hospital once a year for a medical checkup. The Vietnamese were suspicious, but by then Milner held real sway in the Health Ministry and had saved a lot of lives among the country's elite. He insisted: he wanted to study the differences in cancer trouble between them and Orientals. 'That was real gold in cancer studies,' he said. 'Differences between races gave a lot of good leads.' So the men were brought in – though under heavy guard."

"But Paul, why would they keep these men?" asked my wife. "I mean, we're talking about more than a hundred, right?"

"Estimates vary, Wanda – and I mean vary *widely*: from a few hundred to more than twelve hundred. The Vietnamese never published a list of the P.O.W.s, and apparently kept an A list of men they ultimately sent back, some six hundred, and a B list that they kept in reserve as hostages."

"Then imagine the cost of maintenance, health care, keeping them under guard. Why not just give them back to us and say to hell with you? Or just kill them."

"Oh, there's surely a good answer to that, old love," I said. "The men were kept as trophies of their glorious victory. The bloody communists *love* glory. As to upkeep, dispersed across the country as they were, the men receiving the absolute minimum of maintenance, costs were nearly nil. And if what happened to Americans is what happened to Frenchmen after *their* war, it seems that in the long term some men were allowed to marry and live in villages."

Wanda: "Uh-huh. And probably, long term, the men slowly died off, I suppose."

"Yes, they did," Paul continued. "At first Milner kept records on more than a hundred, some brought in from Laos, but the number fell every year, often as not to cancer-related trouble; between 1998 and 2002 the number dropped by nearly half, and soon they were down to a dozen. Some of these had married and lived on communes, though always under the military's thumb. Only two, who had tried to escape several times, were confined to a cell on a military base where they maintenanced vehicles. By then the yearly reunion of the P.O.W.s was a sort of cheerful get-together where the men, some of them in captivity since the mid-Sixties, spoke what English they remembered and exchanged stories and news they'd heard about the United States. That America had elected a black president astounded them. Usually they were in Hanoi for a week of examinations, and Milner always arranged a small banquet for them on the last night.

"'Last year I asked them how many would go back to the States if they could,' Milner told me. 'I wasn't seriously proposing it, you know, just making the point that they'd all adapted to life in 'Nam and it wasn't so bad. But nearly all of them said they would go back in a minute. I asked why. You haven't seen the place for forty years, I told them. They said, all but three of them, that they wanted to die in their own country. I said that was nonsense: what difference does it make if your bones disintegrate here or there? Two or three said they wanted to see their brothers and sisters. One fellow, a Navy flier, had a son. Fine, but what on earth were they going to talk about? Ten minutes after you arrive, I said, you won't have a word to say to one another. Your lives have unfolded here.

"'But they were adamant: they still wanted to return. I said, All right, you're on. Next year at the examination. It'll take some doing, but I can arrange it. Don't come to the check-up if you don't want to go.'

"It required a concatenation of favors, payoffs, and barefaced lies, but the following year, six hours after arriving for their annual review, eight men plus Dr. John Milner were pushing out of Haiphong harbor on a container ship bound for the port of Gwadar, Pakistan. By the time anyone sounded the alarm, they had transferred in Gwadar to another ship, the *Albert Boyd III*, bound for Newark. Milner had made all the arrangements and paid off the captains of each ship. The second was a smallish refrigerator vessel, Lebanese-flagged, that carried perishable goods. In Gwadar it shipped a thousand pallets of dates from Iran; and in Haifa, Israel, picked up a hundred thousand boxes of avocados and mangos.

"But as the *Albert Boyd* pulled out into the Mediterranean, the captain started receiving alarming messages – first about stowaways, then about terrorists – from every maritime authority in the region. *Dangerous men! Search your ship from stem to stern!* Other ships in the area received the messages too; the captain had inquired. He showed them to Milner, who realized that someone was searching hard for them: not only the Vietnamese, but probably the Americans as well. And Milner feared their intentions, since for both countries the men were an embarrassment: Vietnam for keeping them, America for not demanding to get their men back. Certainly the warning about 'terrorists' did not bode well.

"'Well, this went on for a couple of days as we steamed west,' Milner said. 'And then the captain received a message from the Yankees that a U.S. Navy vessel might want to inspect the ship as soon as it passed the Straits of Gibraltar, and he got cold feet. He gave me back half the bread I'd paid, pulled out a map and –'

"I think I did a double-take. 'I'm sorry; did you say you paid him in *bread?'*

"'No, bread: *money.* Don't you use that expression anymore?'

"And for a moment, I had a glimpse of the time-warp these men were walking through. 'Only in movies set in the Sixties,' I replied.

"'Whatever. The captain showed me a map and said, "Where can I drop you off?" We looked at a map and the solution was obvious.'

"As they neared the Straits of Gibraltar in the early-morning hours, the *Albert Boyd* slowed down, and the crew pulled a long-forgotten rubber dinghy out of some storeroom, inflated it and lowered it into the water, and the nine men crept carefully down a long ladder into it. They couldn't wear life vests because the vests would identify the ship. The bridge radioed the Spanish Coast Guard that they had spotted yet another lifeboat of refugees crossing the Straits, and it was already in Spanish waters. An hour later, a cutter showed up, threw the men some life jackets and towed them into the port in Tarifa."

****

Ram interrupted. He was hunched over, staring at his cell phone. "Oh my god! A water tower out in Alexandria's been hit!"

"That's not even twenty miles away," said Wanda. "This is an upper-class area. I knew we'd be hit eventually."

"The police are on the tail of the terrorists," Ram said.

A silence thick as porridge. I wondered how many such silences had been heard throughout history: the long-avoided recognition that the barbarians were closing in.

****

Ram came out of the house holding a fresh glass, which he began noisily filling with ice. "Thanks for waiting. I just wanted to run a couple of buckets of water, just in case. Anybody want a slice of lime? Paul: go."

"So: what to do?" Paul asked the night sky as if he expected an answer. "I couldn't keep the men at Alvaro's for long, it didn't seem right to alert the naval base, and flinging them on the mercy of the

Spanish government as political refugees would take matters completely out of my control. And if there's one thing that years in government has taught me, it's never give up control of the potato unless it's too hot or too rotten. And lastly, heck, these men had pinned their hopes on the U.S. State Department, and it seemed to me we ought to deliver.

"For the moment, I figured I had a window of two or three days while I charted some course of action. Milner had a few thousand left over from what the captain had returned, and I arranged with Matilda the maid the next day to come and take him down to the town to buy clothes and supplies. I figured out how to heat the swimming pool and told the men to stay inside the walls and not make any noise.

"Then I high-tailed it back to Madrid before my absence became noticeable. I told the night-duty staff, in my best espionage tone, that they were to strike from the records the call from the Red Cross and the one they'd made to me. Then I got on a secure line to our esteemed colleague here, Dr. Max Venable, Donelly Chair in Caribbean Studies, and told him I needed a thorough and immediate education in U.S. P.O.W.s left over in Vietnam – this because I couldn't be sure who might be looking at my home and work computers. Was the issue really as serious as Milner was saying? And of course, a few hours later, Max came though. Why don't you give us a summary?"

"My pleasure, old fruit," I said, straightening up in my chair, "though I was so enjoying your narration. Well! Have to sing for my supper a bit. Let me see..."

"Oh, god, here it comes, everybody," said Wanda. "My husband the professor. Pour yourselves new drinks."

"Thank you, my love. Your confidence overwhelms." I sipped my port, complimented Ram on its excellence, and began:

"It was a bloody sordid business all around. The war ended and prisoners were sent back to their countries. But the gasp across Washington was audible when the Vietnamese handed over a list of but six hundred men. Washington had expected more than double that number. There had never been any accounting on prisoners, you see, as the Geneva Conventions require. For that and many other contingencies, the Vietnamese had a very convenient argument: there had been no formal declaration of war on either side, therefore no legal state of war existed, therefore the Conventions did not apply. The men they captured were not soldiers at all, but criminals and murderers – full stop. And with the war's end, it quickly became clear that they intended to keep the remaining men just to be sure Uncle Sam forked over the money they'd pledged: the famous 3.75 billion. They'd done the same thing with the French before them after the French-Indochinese war, which ended in '54, and the French were paying big wampum till 1971."

"But we didn't," said Wanda. "Gosh. That's disappointing."

I sighed, drank. "And so the whole circus began: the White House saying all known prisoners had been returned, the Pentagon stonewalling every congressional investigation, families of P.O.W.s and M.I.A.s demanding investigations, investigations held, investigations stymied, documents gone missing, documents discovered. A bloody mess. Defectors and refugees from Vietnam, after the fall of Saigon, all described seeing prisoners."

"Well, what did the government say about that?" Wanda asked.

"Generally, that these were people trying to curry favor, trying to gain some extra attention and maybe money."

"God, what a bunch of fuckers."

"There's nobody so effortlessly lubricious, old love, as a bureaucrat covering up a scandal."

"Well, what about when Carter came into office? *He* didn't have any baggage from the war."

"Total stonewall. Wouldn't give the families the time of day. Sent them packing."

"Carter the great Christian – shit," said Ram.

"But what about the letter from Nixon?" asked Wanda. "Didn't the Vietnamese take the U.S. to an international court or something over that? I mean, it's black on white, it's signed, it's official."

I: "A few years after the treaty was signed, there was indeed a high-level meeting between the Yanks and the Vietnamese; some of the same people who had negotiated the treaty were there. The Yanks pressed for the return of all their men, the Vietnamese said it could all be arranged as soon as Uncle Sam paid up – all that in the euphemisms of diplomacy, of course. The Vietnamese – no longer the North Vietnamese, now that they had reunited their country – waved a copy of Nixon's letter at the Americans and said, 'What about this, gents?' The reply was that they did not consider that document binding."

"Unbelievable," said Wanda. "Just unbelievable."

"Better tell them about Garwood," said Paul. "That's when I realized what kind of mess these men were in – not to mention myself."

"Indeed, old man. Another tawdry little anecdote. One fine day in 1979, the BBC reported a note from a live American P.O.W.. It had been smuggled out of Vietnam by a representative of the World Bank, gent from Finland. Here was living proof: American P.O.W.s were still alive. Big embarrassment for the Vietnamese, and a headache for the Pentagon."

"Just one guy is a headache?" asked Wanda.

"The problem was not the man, old love, but what he might might have seen, for example, other P.O.W.s. And indeed he had. Private Robert Garwood, U.S.M.C.. A truly gobsmacking story if you ever get the chance to read him up. Long story short, he –" I stopped. The Lilliputians were staring at me. "'Gobsmacking' – *astonishing,* you bloody baboons."

They all laughed. I soldiered on:

"Long story short, Garwood was captured in '65, tortured like all the rest of them, and sent to jungle prisons. Oh, he went through hell, that poor man. American bombs fell on one of his prisons and he was deaf and blind for some six months from the blast. Anyway, early on, an older prisoner took him under his wing and told him the facts of life: either you make yourself useful to the Vietnamese or they let you die. And you can't make yourself useful unless you know the language. He taught Garwood Vietnamese, taught him what to eat out in the jungle to supplement the bit of rice his captors vouchsafed him, showed him what roots would cure cuts and aches – all that. This good man, by the way, was later beaten to death by the guards for some infraction of the rules: just goes to show you what Garwood was up against.

"But Garwood ultimately gave his captors just enough rope to hang themselves with. He made himself useful. He was a farmboy from Indiana, one of these fellows who can fix a tractor with a piece of wire and a wad of gum. And he became their handyman – repaired whatever they brought him: abandoned equipment, rifles, radios, trucks.

"After some years, they took him into Hanoi from time to time to repair things there, and he worked a deal with his guards: they let him go into a high-class hotel – no Vietnamese allowed – and buy cartons of American cigarettes for them to sell on the black market; all he wanted was a pack for himself. Twice he was able to slip foreigners a note with his name and so on. The first time the fellow who got the note informed the Pentagon. It held a meeting among a lot of generals who mulled it over, rubbed their necks, and said, 'No, couldn't be. An impostor. Kids playing a joke.' And they buried the matter."

"Those shits!" cried Wanda.

"Shits indeed, old love. But military men are the same the world over: the lower ranks are all excellent fellows, but theirs is but to do or die. At any rate, the second time around, Garwood passed his note to the Finn there in the hotel lobby and talked to him briefly. And the Finn played his cards right. Rather than going with the note to the Yankees, he got back to London, where he was based, and went with it to the International Red Cross. They wisely passed the note to British media, and then there was no wiggle room for the spin doctors: here was a live American P.O.W. being held against his will who wanted out."

I sipped my port and appreciated its smoothness. "Poor Garwood. Part two of his nightmare was just beginning. He went back on an Air France flight and as soon as it cleared Vietnamese airspace he was charged by American officials with collaboration and some lesser crimes against other prisoners."

"What?" cried Wanda.

"Fuck. Me," said Ram.

"It was so outrageous, not to say *gobsmacking,* that the French captain of the plane came back into the cabin and told Garwood that the plane itself was French territory and he was in command; he would set Garwood down in Paris if he wanted. Garwood said no. He would go back and face the music."

"But why would the military do that?" said Wanda. "That's criminal!"

"The point was to discredit him, old girl. This way, anything he had to say about left-behind P.O.W.s would smack of sour grapes. Garwood was court-marshaled, a few of his fellow prisoners were brought in to testify that he'd collaborated with the Vietnamese prison officials against the prisoners, and it was only the last-minute chance intervention of an Army buddy of his who saved him from the worst charges.

"So Garwood ended up a free man, but he was tossed out into the street with a dishonorable discharge, losing fourteen years of back pay. He could barely speak English anymore, and ended up working at a gas station. Vietnam-veteran organizations helped him get back on his feet. He campaigned hard in favor of abandoned P.O.W.s, but the charges and the media coverage had blackened his reputation. Later on, in the Nineties, Senators John Kerry and John McCaine – both Vietnam vets – buried the evidence on left-behind P.O.W.s – got it all classified Top Secret. Maybe our grandchildren will be able to read the true story."

****

The distant blare of a police siren made us all jump, then laugh at each other.

"So what did you do, Paul?" asked Wanda.

"Well, after talking with Max and mulling over his excellent research" – sitting, he bowed to me – "I figured the lesson was clear: don't go to the Pentagon with the men, but to a news outlet, as that Finnish gent had: that is, first put out the news, and only *then* produce the men. Hand the generals a sort-of *fait accomplit*."

"Which as you all surely notice," I added, "was an extremely risky step for a mere State Department Foreign Service Officer to take. It could well mean the end of his career and maybe his life. But was our friend daunted? Not a bit. He takes his role as a public servant very seriously, and he was going to serve these men come hell or high water." I raised my glass. "To Paul and the rare few like him."

We had to wait for Wanda to run to the bar for a refill, but then everyone raised their glass. "To Paul!"

Paul smiled weakly. "Anyway, I contacted a network reporter stationed in Madrid. There were –"

"Why didn't you go to an Internet website?" Wanda interrupted.

"Well, I thought of that briefly, but you have to remember this was 2010 and alternative news sites weren't so well developed as they are now, and their audiences were small and splintered. And anything controversial appearing on an Internet website automatically has the whiff of 'conspiracy theory' around it. I needed to reach a wide audience with a solid story and generate immediate emotional impact – before the Pentagon could react – and clearly network television was the best medium for that. Does anyone remember Lisa Holliday?"

Nobody did.

"Well, that's not surprising. Female network correspondents all burn out pretty fast when they start looking maternal. Lisa was the usual: thirtyish and ambitious and friendly in that sort of professional way reporters have. She had mountains of hair, big dark eyes, and that tang of sexy TV glamour. I remembered that she hadn't studied journalism but public relations, and had started her career twelve years earlier as a flak for an amusement-park chain." He raised his eyes to heaven. "I swear, what an empty head she had. It took me a good ten minutes to explain about the Vietnam War – she'd heard about it – the abandoned P.O.W.s, Nixon, Garwood, and the present situation. Oh, what a mistake!" Paul moaned. "By the time I'd finished, I knew I'd picked the wrong person: Holliday was seriously intimidated. We were sitting in a café, and the shock on her face must have been clear from across the room.

"When I'd finished, she hesitated so long that I thought her mind had wandered. Finally, she said, 'Are you sure these guys are, like, for real? Like I mean, real dyed-in-the-wool war detainees from Vietnam?'"

I chuckled: Paul always had a fine ear for mimickry.

"'I looked up some of their names on the Vietnam Veterans Memorial web page, Lisa. They're there. One or two of them have lost most or all of their English. Other men translate for them when I say something.'

"'Oh, come on. You never lose your native language. It's like your right arm.'

"'No, it's possible. But imagine how long it takes to get that way.'

"She took this in, fussed with her coffee for a time and then blurted, 'Holy fuck...*fuck!*' Her eyes burst wide open. 'This is like....I mean, like, this really takes it to another level from the cat-stuck-in-the-tree story. It's like a little hard to take all this in at once, you know. I mean, there's research to do, and I'll have to feel out my producer, and....Oh wow, oh boy.'"

Paul closed his eyes in pain. "I should have told her to forget the whole thing right there, and I bet she would've. But the only other full-time correspondent in Madrid was some choir boy from a conservative network, and I didn't trust him. Also, a television reporter is only as good as her producer, and I thought perhaps the producer would steer her along the right paths. I said, 'Lisa, can I give you a hint on how to proceed?'

"'I'd sure appreciate it!'

"I asked who her producer was: not a name to me. So I asked how old he was, and the answer – I don't remember it – at least gave me hope. 'First, send a one-page bare-bones of the story to your producer: *I have a solid source that says that nine American P.O.W.s have escaped Vietnam after forty years captivity and are here in Spain willing to give me their story.*'

"Holliday was breathing heavily. 'Yeah, that's good: *a solid source.*'

"I explained a few other elements for her letter – she recorded them talking into her cell phone – and she said that she would get back to me in a couple of days. I told her that she could not mention me as a source – not even to her producer – and she agreed. Good enough.

"The next day was Saturday, so I headed south on the first high-speed train out and went to Zahara de los Atunes to pick up the men. I wanted to move them some place closer to Madrid. I rented a comfortable mini-bus in Malaga and headed for Zahara. And then as I drove, I heard the news on the radio: the day before, the *Albert Boyd III* had been sunk at sea – went down with the whole crew."

"Shit!" shouted Ram.

"Oh my god!" cried Cindy.

The cries of shock were so loud that the neighbor beyond the fence poked his pasty-white face over. "Ram, did something happen? Did you hear anything?" he asked, and the fright quivered in his voice like a flame.

Ram assured him that all was well: "Our friend is just telling us a ghost story."

"Heck of a time for that," the man grumbled. "Okay, it's just that with that water tower they laid down, the wife and I are a little on edge. And now somebody is trying to hold some California congressman hostage in his house. SWAT team called in, all that."

We got more drinks, and Paul went on:

"Officially, the sinking was the work of that useful, one-size-fits-all suspect: al Qaeda. The ship had been two days away from Newark when the two explosions went off a little after three o'clock in the morning; the ship went straight down, before anyone could get off more than a basic SOS. It sank in more than five thousand meters of water, the deepest part of the North Atlantic west of the Azores. Recovery was impossible; even a superficial investigation would take years."

"It was as murderous as it was clever," I added. "Small ship carrying nothing more dangerous than a bit of produce, Lebanese flag, none of the major carriers involved, ship's crew a dozen Filipinos and Mexicans commanded by three Egyptian officers: pay off the families, file the report, no one makes a fuss. Two torpedos from a Navy sub and nobody's the wiser."

Paul: "Qaeda's message claiming responsibility added that it would now attack any ship carrying Israeli goods. Maritime authorities assumed that the explosives had been put on board well beforehand in Gwadar."

"Jesus. Did you tell the nine men about it?" Cindy asked.

"Yes, but not immediately. I had lunch with them when I got to Zahara, and I had to think it through. It seemed to me that something that drastic meant the Pentagon was four-square opposed to any men coming out of Vietnam, and I had to move carefully. Of course, the upside was that they thought the nine men had still been on board and were now eliminated. So I had time to get things done.

"At lunch I got to hear the stories of two of the other men. We were all spread out with our plates around the living room, the kitchen, and the poolside. I found himself with a small grinning Italian, Tony Rosetti, who had lost all his English and, I realized slowly, some bit of his sanity: he constantly fiddled with his new T-shirt, pulling it down tighter, or drawing it higher up the back his neck. The man translating for him was the black man, Mark McAnder. The fourth man at the table was one of the two imprisoned mechanics that Milner had mentioned. Kyle Harris intended to "shout to the highest heaven" that Vietnam had kept him and others captive and that the U.S. had done nothing about it. A bitter man: pale blue eyes and a lipless craggy mouth. He had lost two fingers of one hand, which he waved around as he talked. It gave me the willies. He told me about his attempt with his colleague to get a message out to pilots flying over.

"'So what kills vegetation the best? You got it: oil – used motor oil,' he explained in his muddy Philadelphia slur. 'Two or three months Danny and me, lugging a bucket every week out of the base to dump it in a pit we'd dug. But instead o' dumpin' it there, little by little, we poured it out in this one field where there was an old dry rice paddy. We spelled out a message: HARRIS SMITH 3-67. Fuckin' twenty-foot-tall letters. Walkin' past, you'd never see it. But a surveillance jet, or a spy satellite? Couldn't miss it. They knew we'd been taken together in March 1967. And they'd come get us. 'Cause like I say, there was no use tryin' to escape: we learned that the hard way. Four attempts, and all we got for 'em was a beating. You run through the fields in 'Nam, and you're this six-foot-tall white guy from Philly, whaddaya expect? And the locals, man, they hated us and they reported us every time. Another attempt was out of the question.'

"'Cong never saw your letters, like from a helicopter?' asked McAnder after translating for Rosetti. He had a singsong Southern accent.

"'Nah – we never had any in our sector: it was all river patrol and trucks. We figured it would take some time – months, maybe a year – but eventually they'd see us and send in the cavalry.' He sneered violently at his plate of chicken. 'Nuttin'. Not a fuckin' thing. Not so much as an airdrop, a flare, an American flag dropped right in the middle of camp that we could wave in the gooks' face. Danny and I used to sit around thinkin' of all the things they could have done to keep our morale up.'

"'The vegetation must have grown back after some time,' I observed.

"'We kept the message clean for nearly four months till the rainy season kicked in.' He giggled bitterly. 'After that, we figured the spy boys had to have seen the message, so we let it get clouded up again before someone happened along on it.'

"'Bad luck,' I said.

"'Bad luck – hah! Wasn't no fuckin' bad luck. More like the Pentagon wanted us good and buried.'"

"Which is probably true," I put in as Paul took a sip of his Cointreau. "I read some books and articles detailing the signs that men were still alive. Dismal reading: several P.O.W.s thought of similar tactics, scratching messages in fields, and recon planes and satellites did indeed sight them. The Pentagon, however, in its wisdom, dismissed them one by one: shadows, coincidence, odd vegetation."

"They ought to be lined up against a wall and shot!" snapped Wanda.

"Indeed, old love. And there was no end to their cynicism. In the years just after the war ended, some American pilots managed to find transmitters called 'PAVE SPIKEs'. They were devices actually dropped all over the countryside, with sensitive electronics to measure troop movements and send the information to satellites or whatever. A pilot happening on one could enter his four-digit PIN number. Through the years, about twenty men did that. Nothing was ever done, though, the report classified."

"Those cocksuckers," muttered Ram.

"There was also Vietnamese radio chatter about American P.O.W.s. But it was intercepted from Thailand, and the Thais, well, they had the best intentions but were probably just trying to curry favor with the American paymasters, weren't they? And they really were a bit amateurish anyway. Even worse, one Secret Service man reported overhearing President Reagan, George Bush (then vice-president), and CIA director William Casey discussing a straightforward offer from the Vietnamese: four billion dollars for the remaining prisoners. The offer was never accepted, though Reagan was apparently sympathetic."

"God, what a shame," Ram said. "People would have given twice that amount if they'd only known. You could have passed the hat at schools, sporting events, churches, supermarkets. Wouldn't have taken a week."

We were silent a while; some of us pulled on jackets.

"The other man I talked to was more interesting," said Paul. "I mean the man from Georgia, McAnder. He had white hair and a beautiful face, skin like an historic old sepia-colored photo, and spoke with the humble cheer of a man who found the bright side of any situation. One of his top teeth and two of the lower were missing from his smile, but all the same it had a kind of lovely saintly appeal.

"'Around the middle Eighties, woulda been, when I met my wife,' he told me. 'Mother o' God, you sure lose track o' time out there. Got knocked around for years, doin' all kinds of jobs, just survivin', pickin' up the lingo. Couple years on, I knew no one was comin' for us. Then ten-twelve of us guys were in this one police jail in Hanoi – two other Americans, the rest Vietnamese hard cases, coupla murderers, from what I could figure. They're holdin' us for distribution up north, ya know. And one day this big ol' police truck...Hell'd they call those things? *Paddywagon* – that's it. This paddywagon pulls up and all of a sudden the cops are all laughin' their heads off. Open up the back, and a bunch o' girls get out. Prostitutes – prostitutes picked up offa the city streets. Sorry-lookin' bunch, that's for sure: bruises, bleedin'. One girl had a dislocated shoulder and between me and another guy we set that to rights. Ya learn to do a lot o' your own medicine there, y'know.

"'Well, the cops shove 'em in with us and let us deal with 'em. Week or so later, Army figures we've all got our girl picked out and they haul us up to a valley – way the hell up north near China. There'd been a war 'tween China and Vietnam up there in the late Seventies, see: bombed-out craters and busted-up villages. Villages are built along the highways, ya know. And they say, Okay, this is where ya live. One man and his girl to a village and God help you if you try an' communicate or run for it. Build your own house. And while you're at it, re-build the town.'

"'And one of the girls became your wife?' I asked.

"'Well, there was no ceremony, but yeah, that's about it. Fine girl, Naavi. Big ol' smile – see it a mile away. Careful about money, good mother, happy with what she had, which was damn little. Made a Christian of her too, and the kids – all on the QT. No church, no priests or nothin'. But I baptized 'em, told 'em all about Jesus and how He lived in our hearts, how He helped me through some goddamn miz'ble times.' The gappy smile appeared as he remembered. 'Good kids, all three of 'em. Good hearts.'

"He pulled a rice-paper envelop out of his shirt pocket and very carefully, as if they were babies, slid out four postage-stamp-sized photos, the kind you would use for a driver's license. The three children, all in early adulthood, had dark complexions and curly hair, but that seemed to be all of McAnder's contribution. None smiled, and the photos had no charm at all. But they meant the world to McAnder.

"I said something neutral. Rosetti and Harris, I noticed, had already seen them, and scarcely glanced over.

"'Naavi died a couple years ago, it'd be now – I think she always had some kinda heart condition. Faded away over about a week. Fine lady. Miss her.'

"'I'm sorry to hear it. My condolences.'

"McAnder wiped away a tear. 'Thank you. Yeah, a fine lady. Hard to communicate with her at first because she was from some place over near Laos: different dialect, y'know. Once our kids were old enough, they caught on, explained a lot of words to me – kind of a game we used to play in the evening, y'know. I taught 'em English just to keep my own intact – on the QT, of course. You don't want the neighbors talkin' 'bout that. The boy, Vang, did pretty well for himself. Knowin' English, he got himself a good job in the Air Force 'cause he could translate training manuals. Last word was he was tryin' out for air-traffic controller down south in Saigon. Got hold of a Bible down there too, kinda filled out his understandin' of the Lord. Haven't laid eyes on him for two years now: he's gotta be careful, y'know. The kids knew all 'bout coverin' up who their dad is once they moved out. The girls both married, had their kids. One's still there, couple o' villages up the valley, other's down around Hué. Husband does road construction.'

"I asked him if he'd seen other American prisoners.

"'Oh, you bet I did,' he said with an alert jerk of the head, making his bit of wattle under the chin shiver. 'Our road was the main one goin' north to China. All the trucks used to gas up at our village before headin' north. And goddamn if ever' so often there wasn't a dozen white guys in ragged black pijamas get out of a truck to stretch their legs, all of 'em chained together at the ankle. Used to, anyway; haven't seen any for a good ten years now – more, maybe. Oh, they looked miz'ble: thin as rails, sores on their skin, ragged beards, hair like a big ol' bush.'

"'Those were the tough-guy prisoners,' Harris put in. 'The gooks really had it in for them. If you didn't cooperate under interrogation when you were captured, they put the label on you, and that stayed with you all your life.'

"'Did you ever talk to them?' I asked McAnder.

"His face crumpled as if at a bad smell. 'Now, Paul, I ain't that kind o' fool. Last thing I needed was trouble. Told my kids too: you see those men – or some tourist comin' through town – you don't know a word of English, hear? One thing you don't wanna do in 'Nam is stand out. You wanna be one more face in the crowd and nothin' else. I told my kids the place to stand out is in school – 'cause that's where you get ahead. Or with your neighbors, helpin' 'em out. My girl Phuong – the one up the valley from me? – she took in a little baby when her neighbor died and the father ran off. Treats her like her own daughter to this very day. That's a Christian lady right there.'

"I asked about Rosetti, the one who'd lost all his English, who through all of this just grinned and ate. McAnder told me that Rosetti was an Air Force navigator that had flown on B-52 bombers. He'd been shot down in 1966 and badly injured; this probably accounted for his slight lunacy. He had spent his whole prison life in Hanoi working as a carpenter and plumber putting in new fixtures for new military installations, which apparently had been his work in America.

"'Here, let me show you somethin',' said McAnder, and called into the living room: 'Captain, throw me that tape measure.' From the coffee table, a man tossed the boxy device to McAnder. 'We were havin' some fun with this yesterday,' he told me.

"He took the tape measure and walked across the room. The men at the other tables looked up and applauded, shouting in Vietnamese to Rosetti, who grinned broadly.

"McAnder pointed at the long, elegant glass coffee table and said something to Rosetti, who replied instantly.

"'I asked him how long this table is,' said McAnder. 'He says 112 centimeters, maybe 113.' He bent down and stretched out the tape measure. 'Right on the money: 112 and a half.'

"The men cheered. Rosetti grinned and shook his chubby hands together like a boxing champion.

"'Now let's try a long one. Paul, give me hand here.'

"McAnder pointed to the far wall. This time it took Rosetti maybe five seconds to answer. I took the end of the tape measure and pulled it to the corner.

"'Perfect,' said McAnder, reading the tape. 'Nine meters twenty-seven on the dime. Man's got an eye you wouldn't believe. We were on that first ship outta Hanoi, y'know, and sometimes Rosetti would point at something and say a number. At first I didn't know what he meant. On the first ship we pretty much had to stay below in our bunks. But on the second one, the *Albert Boyd*, we could move around a little more, and I got hold of a tape measure and tested him out. Couldn't believe it. He's right on the money up to about twenty meters.' He came back to the table and gave Rosetti an affectionate pat on the shoulder. 'Yessiree, all the time these past forty years I've seen how man really is made in God's image.'"

****

The news at this point was that the team of policemen had cornered two of the men who had placed the water-tower bomb; they were in a convenience store, and there were four other people inside. Another man was still on the run. The cornered ones were threatening to blow the place up, and had tossed a grenade under a car on their way in just to ram home the point.

"These guys were prepared," Ram said, hand on forehead as he bent over his phone.

"Bah! It's nothing a another glass of port won't fix," I said. "Paul, old fruit: continue before we all commit hari kari, would you?"

Paul retook his story: "After lunch, I told the men to clean the place up a bit, and they did a far more thorough job than I would have imagined: I supposed it was from the years of keeping up their cells and shacks. They left the place clean as a whistle. Then we hit the road. In the mini-bus, I told them about Lisa Holliday, which cheered them up, and then about the fate of the *Albert Boyd III*, which sobered them immediately. I could hear McAnder behind me choke up as he was translating for Rosetti. I figured that I owed the men the truth, though it hurt like hell to break it to them. For an hour, I could hear McAnder muttering, 'Lord, have mercy on us. Lord, have mercy.'

"Where to leave the men? Well, a few months earlier, Cindy and I had had a good steak lunch in a classic little village of La Mancha – Don Quijote's old stomping grounds? Remember that, Cin'?"

"I certainly do. Casa Pepo, a little inn on the edge of this town: Urda, it was called. You always expect a greasy-spoon-type affair, but you just don't find that in Spain: the linen was as white as snow and the wine glasses spotless. Smashing meat, and the wine – oh my, it's a good thing you were driving." Cindy, I forgot to add, is British like me, though not so phlegmy and thick as your narrator.

"Not much has changed since Don Quijote's time, I can assure you," Paul went on. "Same huddled villages, rocky brown hills, leafy vineyards growing a middle-of-the-road Manchegan wine, here and there olive orchards. On the edge of town, huge three-story steel vats hold the olive oil for distribution. The town church holds the Christ of Urda, a life-sized figure of Christ carrying the cross. It's reputed to have miraculous powers, and people come from all over Spain to pray to it in the church's side chapel. And since praying works up an appetite, a couple of steak restaurants tend to the faithful. They're also hostals with rooms for rent on the upper floors: they cater mainly to weekend hunters. On the side walls of Casa Pepo the features of the hostal are painted in big letters: 'each room with its own television and bathroom.'

"I pulled up at Casa Pepo, showed them my State Department i.d., and inquired about rooms. I told the proprietor, Pepo, that the men were retired friends who had worked in China together for years – that's why some of them liked to speak Chinese. They had been vacationing together down south when their two mobile homes were stolen while they were watching kite surfers in Tarifa. I was getting them new passports and setting them on their feet again — but it would take a few days.

"He had only six rooms, but most had two single beds in them, and he would give the men three squares a day: breakfast, lunch, and dinner. His daughter worked there as well, and she did duty for the hostal's English. Pepo grandly assured me that all his meat comes from the green meadows of Spain's northern coast. The men would eat such steak and lambchops as they had never dreamed of."

"I'm sure they did," said Cindy.

"That done, I took passport photos of the men against a white wall and had them fill out the passport applications that I'd taken from the consulate – and headed back to Madrid."

****

Ram's phone chimed, and he read the bulletin: "The Feds are negotiating with people in the convenience store. But they're warning people to stay inside because they're still looking for the third man. Oh, and in a smaller news item, California, Oregon, and Washington State have announced that they will seek *secession from and a confederation with* the United States. The provisional name is Pacifica. Alaska has also announced that it was seceding from the Union."

"Maybe the governor will offer confederation with Russia," I joked.

"Wow, I never thought they'd actually go and, and do it," Wanda gasped.

"What else?" Ram went on, thumbing his screen rapidly. "In Washington D.C., the president is saying that this isn't a moment for rash action.... blah, blah, blah...the nation has to pull together... blah, blah, blah...terrorism should be our common enemy...and...that's all that's newsworthy."

"It'll all be sorted out before the six o'clock news tomorrow, and Paul's story is a lot more interesting," Wanda said. "So what about Lisa Holliday, Paul? That sounded promising – at least if she talked to her producer."

"Promising – oh god," he said with disgust, looking up to heaven as if it were a waiter who'd spilled soup on him. "I met her the next day, and the moment I entered the café I knew there was trouble. She was sitting in a booth, slapping over the pages of a magazine as if I'd made her wait an hour, which was not the case. I was maybe five minutes late. I'd barely sat down when she rasped, 'They do not want to run the story, and neither do I. Do you think I'm going to accuse the United States Government of not doing everything it could to get our fighting men and women back from Vietnam after the war? What kind of traitor do you think I am?'

"'None at all, Lisa. But that's just the point,' I said. 'The government *didn't* do everything it could. In fact, it did as little as possible, buried the issue, and stonewalled all inquiries.'

"'The whole thing is a lot more complicated than that, Paul. Jack Arnold told me everything that you *didn't* tell me. There was one congressional committee after another that investigated. There were missions into Vietnam looking for guys.'

"Fortunately, by then I'd read up the river of encrypted information that Max had sent me. I came right back at her: 'The committees had no teeth. They were a show. The Pentagon stone-walled them. That's why there was one after another, as you said: because the families of the soldiers kept demanding an investigation worthy of the name. As to missions, they never got off the ground. The only one that did was shot down – literally shot down – shortly after takeoff.'

"This didn't amount to even a scratch on her certainty. 'And that Garwood guy? You *neglected to mention* he was convicted of practically collaborating with the enemy. He fought his dishonorable discharge all the way to the Supreme Court and lost every step of the way.'

"'And those nine rake-thin seventy-year-olds speaking fluent Vietnamese? Now who would they be, Lisa? Someone playing a practical joke on poor little me?' The waitress came and I ordered a cup of tea. Lisa didn't want anything, and I've always felt it was wrong to go to a restaurant and not order, so I ordered a slice of cheesecake, ostensibly for her.

"'I don't know and I don't care,' she snapped as soon as the waitress had left. 'Maybe they were guys collaborating with the enemy, like Garwood.'

"'Which is why they escaped – like Garwood.'

"'Escaped after forty years. Jack Arnold just laughed and said that they can come back with bells on. This is America. We don't do that do people. Most likely, he said, they're geriatric types who never bothered to put money into a retirement fund and now they're looking for a free ride in a high-buck seniors rest home. Or in other words, Paul: who cares?'

"I leaned forward and lowered my voice. 'Who? I can give you at least one answer: the Pentagon. They care, and on a very deep level.'

"'I frankly doubt it.'

"'The ship the men were hitching the ride on in the Mediterranean was the *Albert Boyd III*. Ring a bell?'

"'*That ship that sank?*' Holliday looked at me and pushed one side of her blond hair back over her ears. 'Why the hell would they do that?'

"'Because the generals figured those men were still on board and that sinking the ship was the easiest way to deal with them *and* the crew members they might have told their story to.'

"This actually made her think for a moment. 'Why didn't they just detain the guys long before that?'

"'Well, for some days they were sending stowaway warnings to all the ships in the area. Probably because it took the spies some time to confirm that the men were on board that exact ship. Or maybe the spies needed to talk to people at the port in

Gwadar, Pakistan, where they boarded, or check the surveillance tapes. That would take time too.'

"'Right. And the Pentagon just blew up a whole ship to achieve their immediate objectives, right? Oh, Paul. Now you're getting into conspiracy theories.'

"'Even though the ship went down on the very run that those men were on? Not a week before, not a week after? Even though it sank in the deepest part of the Atlantic and is virtually unrecoverable? It went down so fast that not a single lifeboat could get off. Two huge explosions, according to the pilot.'

"'Tra-la-la-la-la,' she sang. 'Conspiracy, conspiracy.'"

Paul now rose to his feet and raised his glass. "And here, ladies and gentlemen of the jury, let us pause to toast the modern mainstream reporter: whatever doesn't conform to their narrative is conspiracy. If *they* find the facts, they're pertinent. But if some independent journalist publishes another version of events on an Internet website, however well-researched and -documented, *that's* conspiracy theory."

"To the modern reporter," I said, lifting my cup of port. "Sod the lot of them."

"To the modern reporter!" the others sang.

We drank, and Paul sat down again.

"Holliday scooted out of the booth before too much truth could be thrown in her face. 'Bottom line, Paul, is I need to control my destiny and a story about a bunch of old coots who haven't eaten well just doesn't scan on the American radar. Like Jack Arnold told me, "Tell your source to write a fucking book about it if he'll feel better," though I'll tell you right now Paul, it'll have to be a half-assed self-published thing on Amazon.'

"'I'll do that,' I said, 'And in it I'll be sure to record how I brought this story to a major network – no names, please – and it turned me down.' She went off in a huff – good riddance. The cheesecake when it came, though, was terrific: lots of whipped cream on top, with strawberry jam."

****

Paul knocked on his head as if it might be hollow. "I was probably a fool to try another reporter, but I did. I knew several journalists when I was at the embassy – saw them at diplomatic cocktail parties – and they often called to confirm information. If I could, I helped them out. So I called a man who covered southern Europe for a major American newspaper. A kind of dealer in favors: if he passed you the salt, he would figure you owed him one. But at least he was a stickler for getting the details of a story right. I told him I had a unique story – political, human interest, poignant – that he'd be interested in. He was in Marseilles and could be in Madrid the next day for a late lunch – which is no problem in Spain because a lot of people don't have lunch until three o'clock.

"I waited by the glass doors of the restaurant, and Daniel Garon got out of the taxi, sticking the receipt in his wallet. Then he stood there with the door open and his carry-on case on the sidewalk for a full five seconds, staring into the interior of the taxi. I didn't realize what he was doing until he leaned in and checked the floor: he was making sure he hadn't left anything behind. He was a seasoned traveler.

"We settled down in this classy businessman's restaurant a few blocks down from the embassy. Garon had frizzy hair and kept it close-cropped, face smoothly Jewish and agreeable, although he had puffy bags under his eyes that were sagging into second bags. The food came quickly because at three-thirty the lunch rush was petering out.

"'Good ol' Spain: but I still don't get how they can have lunch this late,' he said in a Bronx accent that laid like smog over his words. He had a broad, flat mouth that merely widened a bit more for his smile.

"'People have a second breakfast at about ten-thirty.'

"'Zat so?' he said with genuine amazement.

"'Sure. At that hour, places like this are full, with waiters running full tilt. The best thing is the toast with a garlicky shredded tomato on top.'

"We dug into our lunches, and when we came up for air, he said, 'Paul, if you don't mind, before we get on to your news: have you heard anything about this powuh struggle about the CIA and the

Joint Chiefs? Any good dirt I can use? Been cha-sin' down leads for a month but it's like tryin' to grab fog.'"

Paul stopped and raised a hand. "Which I ought to fill you all in on, since it forms a small part of my story. There was a move at the time to reorganize the U.S. intelligence community. The CIA reports to the Director of National Intelligence, right? Well, the proposal was to eliminate the DNI altogether, put the CIA in its place, and that *all* intel organizations would report to them. This, of course, would have given the 'Company' a higher profile and no small power over – you guessed it – the *Defense* intel agencies. And you can imagine what the Joint Chiefs had to say about *that.*

"Well, the fight was on. A miniature war erupted, each side trying to make the other look bad. For example, I'd heard that a Navy ship was supposed to pick up a couple of CIA guys who'd been exfiltrated from somewhere in Siberia and dropped in the northern Pacific; but the ship took its time about it, and the guys on the lifeboat froze their butts off waiting. And there were rumors that the CIA was withholding intel on one thing and another, and as a result some Marines in Somalia had walked into an ambush. Things like that."

"Bureaucratic infighting, with the accent on the fight," I mused into my drink. "Seems to me I've heard of that."

"Anyway, I gave Dan Garon a few tidbits I'd heard around the embassy, namely that the military attachés would scarcely exchange a word with the CIA head of station, a gruff old guy called Gormley who a few weeks before had flat-out asked me whose side I was on. More on him later.

"Finally we got down to brass tacks. We were on our after-lunch café-con-leche then, and Garon reached into a satchel he carried and pulled out a broad notebook. He laid it on the table and flipped its cardboard flap up and onto the table. Then he slashed a few pages forward until he found a clean one. 'Well, so much for shop talk. Whaddaya got for me, Paul?'

"'The Vietnam War. Long and terrible, lots of protest, finally ended in 1973, right? Well, you may or may not remember that in the years *after* the war, there was a lot of controversy about whether or not North Vietnam – later just plain Vietnam – had returned all the American P.O.W.s it had.'

"Garon pulled his long mouth into a frown as he thought. 'Yeah, tickles a few tumbluhs back there. Vietnam, huh? Sure wasn't expectin' *this.*' Garon motioned with his coffee cup. 'But go on, ya nevuh know.'

"'Washington expected more than a thousand prisoners would be returned, and only about six hundred came back. Vietnam said that was the whole lot. And the White House and Pentagon said the same thing: it's all over, nothing to see here.'

"'That's right – I remembuh dat,' Garon said cloudily. 'Later on, Clinton...yeah, *Clinton* restored relations with Hanoi, they returned remains of

U.S. personnel, everything hunky-dory like we'd nevuh fired a shot there. Now they're a trading partnuh, and they're playin' the neutral game between us and the Chinese — tryin' to steer an even course. Not goin' too well lately, what with China growin' and investin' there. Okay.' He slid a pen out of his shirt pocket and wrote *Vietnam* on the blank page of his notebook. 'Go on.'

"'Okay, a few days ago I stumbled across some concrete information about the P.O.W. controversy.'

"Garon wrote *P.O.W.s* and with one hand and sipped coffee with the other. You could see he'd interviewed a lot of people this way. 'About the P.O.W.s not returning, you mean.'

"'Right.'

"Garon folded his arms and considered. 'Is this infuhmation somethin' that you *saw* or that someone showed you or told you about?'

"'That I saw. That I *have*. Proof positive.'

"'That's good, very good.' Garon examined me carefully. 'As long as we're talkin' proof that all the P.O.W.s were *returned*.'

"'No, the opposite: that a great many were left behind. I've got nine of them who recently escaped after forty years, and they'd love to tell you their story.'

"'*You* got them?'

"'Figure of speech. They washed up on a Spanish beach in a raft, having jumped ship as the vessel sailed through the Straits. The Spanish Red Cross called me, I went down there, and that's what I found: nine men, and over the years they've seen a lot more Americans left behind. For the moment, nobody knows about them. I've put them up in a town near Madrid.'

"Garon finished his coffee and reached for his notepad. He brought up the cardboard cover up to vertical and let it fall shut with a puff. A grave sigh. 'Paul, first of all, I'm grateful that you called. You were thinking you had a fabulous story for me, and I appreciate it. My treat fuh the lunch okay? The papuh gives me a sweet expense account. But I can tell you right now my boss is not going to run no story that says America left her boys behind in 'Nam. Fuhgeddaboutit.'

"'How do you figure?' I griped. 'If this doesn't fall under *All the news that's fit to print,* what does?'

"'Well, that's the *Times,* but the same applies to us. The operative word there is "fit." And believe you me, this isn't *fit* for a lotta reasons.'

"I couldn't keep the anger out of my voice. 'Please enlighten me, Dan, so I don't make you come all this way the next time.'

"Garon caught the waitress's eye, wrote a figure in the air, and put away his notebook. 'First, it makes the papuh – the media in general – look bad for not finding out the truth to start with. But second, like I say, it isn't *fit.* It doesn't fit the narrative: that in our democracy every person counts, which in this case means the government wouldn't ever knowingly leave its fighting men behind as prisoners. Look, a newspapuh or a newscast is a story, and everything has to fit: the rise and fall of sports teams, the weathuh, elections, foreign wars. It can have a few loose ends, yeah, but very few. If we're always saying, "Whoops, sorry, here's somethin' we missed," people don't trust us. Fuh bettuh or worse, we give some kind of form, some shape, to life, to reality beyond your front do-ah.'

"'But if you don't present a loose end now and then, your cred suffers, doesn't it? I would say, in fact, that one of the things that makes people distrust mainstream news and look at alt media is just that: the news is too smooth, it doesn't present any loose threads, it doesn't go back and say, "Whoops, sorry, here's something we missed, and it's one hell of a scandal." That's just good policy.'

"'All right, yeah, point taken. But at most the scandal would have to be somethin' like...like a Watuhgate or Russiagate or the Clinton sex scandals – things that can be handled through the normal channels of investigative reporting and only entangle the stars of our show, like presidents and senatuhs, maybe a celeb' or two. To publish that the Pentagon left twistin' in the wind guys who'd answered the call of duty involves, *one,* an institution, and *two,* normal people.' He sat back and folded his arms again. 'Outta bounds – outta bounds by a mile.'"

A low growl issued from Paul's throat that startled us all. "It was this Bhudda-like certainty that nauseated me: this guy from the Bronx shaping reality for a whole country. I said, 'Sounds like an Orwellian novel to me, Dan.'

"'And we're the good guys in it,' said Garon, laying a gold-colored credit card on the lunch bill. 'You mentioned alternative news websites. Look at what they're foistin' on society: schizophrenia. Nowadays you got people say reality is A, others say B, and others C. Why? Because we don't have a single, coherent story-telluh anymore. That's us, the mainstream guys. Yeah, yeah, we get a few things wrong – no argument. Even a few *big* things. Believe you me, though: history will thank us as being one of the few forces tryin' to hold society togethuh.'"

Paul sipped his Cointreau and shrugged. "Well, that's how he saw himself, and I wasn't going to change his mind over lunch. I left the gratitude to history and said, 'That's pretty cold consolation to any issue that's off the media grid – like these nine men I'm trying to get home. And I've got to get them some publicity in order to do it. Otherwise, the Pentagon will try to bury them.'

"He weighed this. 'Yeah...Yeah, it is what it is. Sounds to me like you gotta look for a different strategy. Hey, what kinda tip can I leave for the lady?'

"It took me a second to realize the conversation was over. 'Five euros will do.'

"'Great. Tipping's highway robbery in Manhattan these days: drop less than twenty percent and the fuckin' maitre d' runs aftuh you down the street. All I've got is a ten. Well, let's make her day.'

"On the street, he flagged down a taxi and turned to shake my hand. 'Paul, again my thanks: you were thinkin' o' me and I don't forget a favuh when someone....' Then he brought a forefinger to his lips as if he were telling me to stay quiet. But he was thinking, the dark eyes squinting. Then his finger swung down and pointed at me. 'Yeah, this might work...this might actually work. Paul, take this business to your CIA head-of-station here. 'Cause I'll bet you our next lunch – and you can throw in a bottle o' Dom – that the Company would *love* to beat the Pentagon ovuh the head with a story like this. They maybe might want to re-jigguh the narrative around, make it look like *they* discovuhed the guys in 'Nam and brought 'em home, whatevuh, but it's right up their alley. They're probably as neck-deep in shit about the prisoners as the Pentagon, but they'd jump at the chance to present themselves as the white-hats on this thing....Yeah, try it out. Even then, the whole thing might stay unduh bureaucratic wraps and nevuh make the news – probably won't, in fact – but the Company would give your boys covuh when they reach E Pluribus Unum.'

"With that, he threw his carry-on and satchel onto the back seat, checked around the sidewalk in case he'd dropped something, and got in."

****

"How many of these have I had, Cindy?" Paul asked his wife, who had refilled his glass.

"Enough to be fluent, dear. You're doing wonderfully well."

"Yeah, get on with it, Paul," called Ram as he returned to his hammock. "I'm starting to wonder if you're gonna adopt these nine guys as your sons."

"Anything on your cell, Ram?" Wanda wondered.

He checked. "No – Twitter chatter: couple guys saying the world is ending...others say it's a new beginning" – he grinned – "and a couple literary types who say that every ending is a beginning. There! Paul, keep talking. What happened next?"

"Well, dear listeners, hat-in-hand I walked up to the fifth floor of the embassy, genuflected to the security man, and sat down in the office of Craig Gormley, our head-of-station, and explained my story across yet another table to yet another bemused face." He drank.

"First, what can I tell you about Craig Gormley? If you can imagine a campaign advance man or a Chicago commodities trader whose numbers are turning south on him, you have Gormley: tie pulled down, half a shirt tail flapping behind him, big head of hair hanging out in bits and branches. The funny thing was that now and then he got a haircut, and he looked ridiculously neat for weeks until his hair grew out again. Now and then you would hear him arguing on his cell phone with one of his ex-wives or maybe one of his sons who had slugged another teacher. Otherwise, he kept up a steady drumming of his thumbs on his cell phone, and talked to you without looking up. He knew everything happening across the face of the earth and still wanted more.

"As I talked, his bushy head would jerk up from the phone and he'd stare at me, muttering, 'Yeah, you're connecting some dots for me,' and drop his head again. And when I'd finished: 'So *that's* why the Vietnamese are suddenly moving their checkers around. Well, I'll be damned: old P.O.W.s.' He went back to his phone.

"I waited. 'Craig, if I've caught you at a bad time, I can –'

"'Time's okay,' he griped. 'Hell's the matter with the time?'

"'You seem...rather busy.'

"A shrug. 'Normal day. Fuckin' Turks throwin' monkey wrenches all over the place again. One of these days we're gonna put on a show there. Oh man, are we ever gonna put on a show.' He turned to his computer screen – which was turned away from me, of course – and began reading it. 'So whaddaya want me to do about your prisoners? This is the CIA, not a Red Cross camp.'

"I waited long enough to make Gormley look up from his fussing.

"'Well?' he demanded. 'Say something.'

"'I'm practicing diplomacy at the moment.'

"'Hell's that supposed to mean?'

"'That I'm on the other side of your desk, Craig, and I'd appreciate it if you would look me in the eye.'

"'Twenty-first century, Klippen. This is how people talk now. Look at a pack of kids on the sidewalk. All facing each other talking over their phones.'

"'So call me old-school.'

"'F'fuck's sake,' Gormley moaned. He turned to me. 'Happy?'

"'No. Turn your phone over so that you can't see the screen.'

"'F' fuck's sake!' But he did.

"'Craig, I actually have something to say that could well be to your advantage. Some time ago, you asked me whose side I'm on.'

"'And you wouldn't say. Fuck you.'

"'No, but the question means that there are two sides and they are enemies. My P.O.W. problem, if you handle it right, could be a baseball bat that you could use on the guys with the medals on their chests.'

"Gormley squinted at me suspiciously as if I might pull a gun on him. 'How?'

"'That Lebanese freighter, the *Albert Boyd III*? The Pentagon had it sunk because they thought the men were on it. Follow me?'

"He nodded. 'Figures.'

"'Which means they're desperate to keep those men in the dustbin of history. But what if they returned to the U.S.? And word got out, whether through the news media or just on the military grapevine, that they'd returned and knew about others left behind? And the Pentagon knew about it too? Hadn't fought for their men years ago? Had participated in the cover-up back in the Seventies and Eighties? That would be a baseball bat that your agency director could swing at Pentagon heads and knock one or two out of the park.'

"I hadn't even finished the sentence before Gormley's hairy head jerked to attention and his hands were rubbing his thighs vigorously. He was running through the contingencies, the scenarios, the narratives, the arrangements. I added at this moment, gasoline on his fire, that I wanted no credit whatsoever in the matter – especially since I'd already exceded my authority. If he could get the men back to the U.S. safely, I would happily give him the reins of the op. Which, of course, to an ambitious CIA man looking to earn points in Langley, was music to his ears." Paul laughed. "In fact, at this moment, his phone vibrated, and he opened his desk drawer and swept it in.

"'Yeah, okay, this has a pulse. This is radar-able.' That was his word: *radar-able*. 'Pentagon knows the men are here in Spain, but –'

"'*They do?*' I blurted.

"'Yeah, 'cept they don't know exactly where. Just Spain. They sent some hardball crew – arrived last night. Four-man hit team, looks like. They're using one of *our* shell offices out by the airport. Dumped enough gear on the floor to build a skyscraper.'

"I immediately thought of Lisa Holliday – or her producer – and Dan Garon. Media people, of course, have links to the military. But I would turn out to be completely wrong." Paul looked heaven-wards again. *"Completely* wrong. Well...

"Gormley was muttering over my head at the wall. 'Fly 'em out in a CIA 12-seater. Clear the flight plan ahead of time. Take a low lane towards Char-lotte and veer off....Get someone to bang the FAA.. Set it up at the last minute before the fuckin' DoD can jump us.'

"'Sounds like the stuff we need.'

"Gormley said nothing, but very slowly pulled his cell phone out and stared at it. 'I'll run it by Langley, see what they say. Question is...the ques-tion *is,* who? Who's going to fast-track this to the A.D.? This has to go forward *now.'* He looked at me. 'The nine men – they're taken care of for anoth-er few days? They can stay put? Nobody but you knows where?'

"'They're fine.'

"'All right. You keep your head down, Klippen: look like your doing some real work around here. I'll let you know.' He began beating his thumbs on his phone; I left without another word."

****

"So I kept busy for a couple of days. I had a meeting with a millionaire Spanish real estate mogul whose cuff links had sapphires big as chestnuts in them. His project on the already overbuilt south coast of Spain had run into a roadblock: the Russian oligarch who was funding it had been hit by American sanctions and couldn't send fresh funds to keep the project going. Could I talk to people in Washington and obtain a waiver, just for the project? Otherwise, sixty-five construction workers were going to be idled, he added with milky sorrow, as if he gave a hoot what happened to them. I said I'd do what I could.

"Then I got stuck with a meeting with a self-important woman who wore her blond hair brushed straight back, the female signature of Spain's imperial class. She was a top name in a parliamentary opposition party. 'We are very angry,' she told me, 'that you are avoiding during six months that we go to the embassy for a frank conversation.' *God help us all if we have to deal with this lady as foreign minister,* I thought. I assured her, lying through my teeth, that the embassy had not tried to put off a meeting, and enjoyed her puzzled frown, knowing that 'putting off,' one of those tricky English phrasal verbs, would put her off her game and make her put off the rest of her attack. English can be a devilish weapon against the non-native speaker."

"Paul can be a little nasty when he wants," Cindy informed everyone.

"My best-informed critic, ladies and gentleman," Paul added, raising his glass to her. "Oh, I also got the men's passports from the embassy consul, who'd rushed them through because the ambassador had signed an order to do it. He signed everything I told him to sign. He got his job because he was a big contributor to the president's campaign, and had the good graces to tell me his first day on the job that he had no idea what he was doing."

"Lucky you," said Wanda drily. "The same thing happens in my department, only the idiot at the top won't admit it."

"Then I talked to Craig Gormley, who informed me that his idea – officially *his*, remember – had gone down with a bang in Langley. Both the assistant director *and* the director were delighted. They planned on a full press conference with the nine P.O.W.s standing behind them. The Pentagon would be informed about five minutes before starting so that they would have their TVs turned on to watch it. I asked Craig if the White House had been informed and approved of all this, and he only answered that those were matters above his pay grade; but he believed so."

"'Believe' – bloody strange word to use about a CIA man," I muttered. "Sorry, old man. Please."

"I know what you mean, Max, but at the time it was better than nothing. Two days later, some CIA people flew in, and there was a big organizational meeting – over-organizational is probably a better word: we spent a half-hour alone arguing about what kind of clothes the men would wear for the presentation. I would pick up the men the next day, drive them to a place in Madrid where they would spend the night, giving them a little briefing along the way. In particular I was to stress that I personally had to remain out of the picture, that the entire operation, from the moment they arrived in Tarifa, had been CIA, which was proud to repatriate our fighting men, whom the naughty Pentagon had ignored completely after the war. The sub-text of the presser, of course, would be, *Yes, good citizens, this is why the CIA deserves to be in control of American intel, because we really have the interests of the average guy at heart, and your reps in Congress can vote for this new structure wholeheartedly.*

"So things were finally looking up for the men. They would go back to America and in such a situation that the Defense Department wouldn't try to silence them – or worse. The next day –"

"Pardon me again, old fruit," I added. "But you're skipping over an important point, as I recall. Another very worthy reason for your putting your career in considerable jeopardy for these men was the ongoing wars in Afghanistan and Iraq. A minor scandal about abandoned Vietnam P.O.W.s, you felt, might make the Pentagon more eager to recover American P.O.W.s left behind in wars present and future."

"Hold on," called Ram. "More news."

The convenience store had been blown to smithereens when snipers hit one suspect and only wounded another. In Oregon, the State Congress was under siege from armed nationalists who did not agree with the declaration of independence. The Oregon National Guard, defying the White House, had fired on the nationalists – many dead – and said that they would defend their freedom. And there were unconfirmed reports that regular Army soldiers and Marines from nearby bases had come to join them, for the numbers of the Guard had swelled noticeably in the last few hours. Heavy artillery was showing up around the city. The president had made a brief appearance, saying, "The Pacific states need to be talked down from the cliff before they do something stupid."

"This is getting *so* ugly," said Wanda.

****

"As I say, if it wasn't a solution, at least it was progress," said Paul. "The next morning I rented another large mini-van and headed south. And then a strange thing happened."

He drank. "The last stretch on the way to Urda is from the town of Consuegra, which has a castle and a series of old-style windmills on a high hill – the kind that Don Quixote tilted at. I saw a tourist bus up there with a lot people taking pictures. Well, it's about four miles from Consuegra to Urda, and about halfway, I passed a black man walking beside the road. It took me a second to realize that it was Mark McAnder. So I pulled over to a lay-by and waited for him.

"'Oh! It's you,' he said. 'Well, praise the Lord, my dogs were really startin' to bark.'

"'Where have you been?'

"'Oh, just out and about.' He jerked a thumb over his shoulder. 'Walked over here to Consuegra this morning, took a look at the castle and them windmills. Figgered it was now or never, since we're headin' for Madrid today. Tour guide said the castle goes back a thousand years – ain't that sump'm? Tenth century. Bit off a little more 'n my legs can chew, though. Ya haven't got a swallow or two o' water there, do ya, Paul?' I handed him my bottle and he drank voraciously. 'Ah, praise the Lord, that's good! Hardly left you a drop, though.'

"'Go ahead: finish it. I bought a dozen bottles for the trip to Madrid.'

"The bus was well off the road, and it was a sunny day – as usual in Spain – with the vineyards bushy with leaves and stretching away to the crest of a red-soil hill. We just sat there talking for a while, turned sideways to each other in the front seats. McAnder told me how much he was enjoying Spain. Every day he had taken long walks, some on the rocky dirt roads running between the vineyards, others on the highways. He waved a hand around and said, 'Feel that, Paul? Air here is so dry – light as a blessin'. In 'Nam it sits on you like a wet blanket. I musta walked halfway to Consuegra this mornin' before I even broke a sweat.'

"'The whole center of Spain is like that. The temperature can be in the nineties, but as long as you're in the shade, you're comfortable.'

"He pointed to the top of the hill and said that from there he had seen a watch tower miles away on top of another hill. 'I guess they used 'em for sendin' messages up and down the country – you know, just with signals that they used. They could send a message from north to south in just a few hours.'

"'Did you hear all that from the tour guide?' I asked.

"McAnders smiled, and even with the gaps in his teeth it was an infectious smile, his face all squished up around his eyes and mouth. 'Well, I made me a kind of friend here: priest there at the church in Urda. Saw me in there prayin' every morning. Heckuva nice guy, speaks a kind of basic English. I guess he went up to London when he was a young man and spent a year workin' at Burger King. Says there's nothin' like it for learnin' a language.'

"'He was probably happy to have someone to practice his English with,' I said, thinking of a few Spanish bores who had cornered me.

"McAnder looked away over the vineyards for a moment and said, 'Say, Paul, I gotta ask ya somethin'. Don't take this poorly, after all you've done for us, but...any chance I could stay on here in Spain?'

"'Stay. You mean, not go back to the U.S.?'

"He raised his broad, thin hand and flapped it at the hills. 'Look. Thing is...I don't got nothin' to return to Stateside, Paul. I got a sister somewhere – that's about it. Harris and Smith, maybe some o' the other guys, they're gonna raise a big stink 'bout us gettin' left behind, but me' – his eyes roved over the fields – 'me, I ain't one for raisin' stinks. Me, I just try to get along. I didn't have a bad life in 'Nam. Made somethin' of it, turns out. Villagers there, me and them built one hell of a school in our town; and then we expanded it ten years later on account of all the kids bein' born. Dug the ditches for the water pipes m'self. My kids all went to school there. Man, there ain't nothin' like watchin' kids soakin' up their lessons, growin', maturin'. My older girl does math problems like a hot knife cuttin' through butter.'

"'Must be very gratifying.'

"'Damn right. Now, when we escaped and all, I was just thinkin' I'd like to live a few years as a free man. V'etnamese military cops was always checkin' up on me like I was some kinda murderer on parole or somethin'. One cop was always shakin' me down, sayin' he was gonna report me tryin' to escape if I didn't put a few bucks in his hand.'

"'There's always one in the crowd.'

"'Well, when the doctor said he'd try an' put somethin' together, I thought, Hell yes: see some-thin' different, see what the U.S. is like now. And okay, maybe I was ready to stick a hot one to the V'etnam government too. I mean, really, the only thing that's kind of stuck in my craw all these years about 'Nam is, y'know, I don't like someone else *tellin'* me I got to live there. Who knows? If I'd'a traveled there and liked it, I mighta stayed. All that jungle and mountains and the like. Beautiful birds, butterflies. Pretty big show for a guy from rural Georgia.'

"'I'll bet.'

"McAnders opened another bottle of water and took a lusty few swallows. 'But, y'see, Paul... between the pretty countryside here and the prayin' I been doin' every day up in that big beautiful church with the statue of our Lord, and the Cross and the paintin' on the walls, well, I'm startin' to wonder if the Lord ain't tellin' me this is the place to be.'

I nodded. "'Well, it's a free country. And I've brought along your new passports.'

"*Hey, really? You think I could?* I was talkin' to Padre Diego, the priest, about it, see, and he told me about this place: big ol' monastery up north coupla hundred miles or so. Monks run it. Quiet place, farm villages here and there like Urda not too far away. I guess they grow their own vegetables a lot of the year, pray twice a day, carry around a Virgin Mary on a kind of float at Easter – big procession with the villagers, I guess. And they make some kind o' fine wine. Sounded pretty good: tendin' the grapes, harvestin', pourin' it all into these big oak barrels. French oak, they use, he tells me.'

"'I've heard of that.'

"'Think I could, Paul? I mean, without you gettin' in a lot o' trouble.'

"'I can arrange something.' And the truth was that I was so happy for him I would have plowed a path right through the Pentagon to make sure he could make it to that monastery. 'Let me give it a think.'

"'Aw, that'd be swell, 'cause when I told Diego we were leavin' today, he gave me this name and telephone number to call.' McAnders was digging in his pocket. 'Said if I could just get my butt up there to this city, the chief monk would come and get me. He called the guy up and he said they'd be happy to have me. All the monks there are gettin' old, I guess. They haven't had a new member in fifteen years. Room and board in exchange for helpin' with the upkeep and the garden and the grape harvest, stuff like that. Thought that might be a pretty good deal.'

"'You'd have to learn Spanish,' I said.

"McAnders grinned again, wrinkles emanating from his eyes and mouth like waves in a pond. 'Diego gave me a couple o' books: a bi-lingual Bible in Spanish and English, and a book on how to learn Spanish. Didn't look too hard: *comunicación* is *communication*.'

"'After Vietnamese, Spanish'll be a snap.'

"I looked at the paper. The city was Medina del Campo. 'Sure. There are lots of buses going that way. It's right beside the major highway going to northwestern Spain. It's where the best Spanish wine comes from.'

"'Sounds like my kinda place.'

"'All right. I'll get you there. Just let me think over the best way to do this. The guys who had your ship blown up aren't going to be too happy about one of you going astray.'

****

"And so," Paul said with a clap of his hands, "to great éclat did I hand out the passports to the men at Casa Pepo. A few of them cried. McAnder received his and said, 'God bless ya, man. God bless ya.' Little Rosetti hugged me. Pepo the restauranteur walked around the room filling wine glasses, and we drank a toast to our new passports.

"Then we sat down for a last lunch – grilled lamb chops, wonderful – though all the while I was mulling over what to do with McAnder. I ate with Dr. Milner and a fellow I hadn't talked to before, a tough old Texan called Captain Jim Clooney – he insisted on being called by his rank: 'After all,' he explained, 'we've never received our discharge; we're still on active duty.' On the men's first ship out of Haiphong harbor he'd had his gray hair shaven to a table-flat crew cut. As far as I ever heard, he was the only one of the men who was glad that the U.S.had never paid ransom for the prisoners."

"Wow. That *is* tough," said Wanda.

Paul sighed, looking at his drink. "Oh, poor Captain Clooney. He'd really gone through hell. He was a granite-hard Navy flier who'd been shot down and captured by the Viet Cong: the Vietnamese Communists who operated somewhat independently of the North Vietnamese Army. Like ideologues everywhere, they were a vicious bunch, and Clooney was treated to every kind of torture known to man – this when they weren't using him for slave labor. For years after the war he lived with other prisoners in a cave where they were used as plow horses, literally harnessed and pulling the blade through the ground for a guy with a whip. He had a crazy quilt of scars and pale skin grafts over his neck, and he could only use one hand to eat because the other shook too much.

"'Worst of it, though? Clearin' those goddamn fields. Mines and unexploded ordnance. Lots of it,' Clooney said. He spoke in spoonfuls of phrases and had never lost his West Texas accent. 'Gooks made us walk 'em. 'Bout ten of us across. Used a li'l flat stick, spatula-like. Good as shit, though. Wet ground, years pass. Damn mines mos' the time invis'ble. Just hadda step lightly and pray. Guys ten feet away from me, *boom*. Blown sky-high. Gooks, they just laughed. Told us to get on with it. Real sons o' whores. I get back to civi'zation, gonna write a book about it. How they treated our servicemen.'

"Milner had finished – he ate very little anyway – and was swirling the wine in his glass and listening to Captain Clooney. And when Clooney reiterated that he was glad that the U.S. had never paid ransom for the left-behind P.O.W.s, he said, 'But it's different for you, Captain: you're a professional military man, enlisted before the war to be a Navy pilot. You were planning on a military career. What about the poor draftee?'

"'How d'you mean, sir?'

"'Very simple. Americans put great stock in not being bossed around by their government. It's their version of freedom. It means the government cannot come to your house and tell you to – what? – paint it orange or tell you to do jumping jacks in the front yard every morning. Isn't that right?'

"'We have *pure freedom* in America, sir,' the Captain said stiffly. 'Not a *version* of it. And no, the government may not tell you to do that.'

"'But it can draft you in time of war – that's in the rules, right?'

"'Every citizen has to defend the nation, yessir.'

"'And I agree. But doesn't that obligation come with a kind of statute of limitations? I mean, once the war is over, the government cannot keep you indefinitely in service. If freedom means any-thing, the government must release you from service once hostilities have ended. And it should do whatever it can, short of starting another war, to secure the freedom of its men who have been left behind.'

"The Captain shook his crew-cut head. 'Risks every soldier takes, sir. Sacrifices we make for the country. Gooks shoulda released us all im-mediately.'

"'Sacrifices made by the professional military man as well as the draftee? That's damned unreasonable. *You* accepted the risks; *they* accepted a limited obligation for a specific conflict.'

"'Soldier serves at the pleasure of the commander-in-chief. Why I never talked: felt the President of the United States standin' right b'side me. Whole time.'

"Milner coughed for a moment in order to hide his smile; yours truly, the veteran diplomat, understands and forgives.

"'No disrespect intended, Captain,' said Milner, 'but I've always thought it was useless not to cooperate once you'd been taken prisoner. Why not talk and save yourself a lot of pain?'

"'Gooks wanted to know secret call codes. They get 'em, deceive our pilots. Give 'em phony coordinates. Lead 'em right to their gun sights and *boom.*'

"'But obviously, Captain, if a plane had been downed, U.S. military planners had to assume that whatever information the pilot had was now compromised, and they had to adjust. So what good was your silence? That's what I always told any captured men that I treated: Don't be a fool; go along with everything. Most of the time, prison conditions were primitive and unsanitary, and in the tropics a beating from prison guards – even just a bad scratch – could be fatal.'

"'Military code of honor – gooks shoulda respected it,' said Clooney. 'Name, rank, serial number and date o' birth. That's all anyone ever got out of me. Okay, except this one time: told 'em what kinda aircraft I flew: F4Bs, big deal; so did half the Navy.'

Milner scowled. "'And besides a beating, what did silence gain you, Captain? A little fuzzy feeling of holiness? Pride? Has your government paid you back with a like loyalty? Even before being taken prisoner, wasn't it clear to you that you were being used as a pawn in their game?'

"'Military code of honor,' Clooney repeated doggedly. 'You wouldn't know anything about that, would ya? By the way, gonna talk to the debriefers. Tell 'em you were urgin' our men to talk. Collaboratin' with the enemy if anything ever was. See what the board has to say about that, huh? 'Scuse me, junnelmen.' And he picked up his plate and walked to another table, then came back for this glass because his other hand shook too much.

"Milner refilled his glass and offered to refill mine, but I would be driving and put a hand over my glass. 'What a goddamn fool. Government just thrives on naive bumpkins like that. And the most naive are the middle-ranking military men. I see it among my elite patients in Hanoi, on the Politburo. A man rises through the ranks – mayor, local secretariat, regional commander – and up to a certain height in government he's a true believer, servant of the people. And then....I don't know what it is. At some point he passes through a kind of religious looking-glass. He's no longer connected to his people; he's connected to his elite. He leaves love and friendship behind, and suddenly he's all pride and prestige. You believe in God, Klippen?'

"'What?' I exclaimed. It was an odd turn of subject. 'Well, if it makes any difference to you: yes,' I answered.

"'I remember reading an anthropologist who'd studied a whole variety of cultures, both modern and ancient. And she talked about how all cultures, no matter how isolated, have some type of religion. She said man seems hard-wired for it.'

"'Sure. You can find religion of some type in the very back of the Amazon or the deepest African jungle.'

"'Just so. Well, I've turned that one over through the years, and I think she got it wrong. God isn't what man prays to, it's what he aspires to: total power, no rules, or make your own rules. I'm not talking about all men, but the more able ones who hear the call and decide to become God. A man rises and rises in his country – government or business – gaining more and more power, and then one day he wakes up and, *poof!*, he's made it: he's God. And below him are the pawns, to be played as necessary. You're a young guy, but you've probably heard about the anti-war demonstrations of the Sixties, right?'

"'Yes.'

"'Roaring city-wide protests against the war, year after year – oh, I remember as a student seeing a veritable *river* of long-hairs marching through the U of Wisconsin campus in Madison.

Burning of draft cards, chants, police whacking kids with batons – all of it. And it didn't change a damn thing. Total waste of time: to those men in Washington in their thin black ties it was the merest rustling of leaves.'

"'I'd be a *little* more charitable: I would say the protest *shortened* the war. Public opinion ran heavily against it.'

"'Maybe. From what I've read, the Watergate scandal weakened Nixon's hand in the negotiations a lot more than the protests ever did. But my point is, some years later I read that Americans were shocked to learn that the Defense Department knew the war couldn't be won – but carried on anyway. According to The Pentagon Papers, the whole military and foreign-policy elite knew it. But they still went on with the war, throwing more pawns into the fire. Why? Because they were gods. The sense of state had replaced the sense of humanity. To listen to the people and their demands would mean they weren't gods anymore.'"

Paul gave us a dark look. "I remembered Dan Garon and wondered if the same thing hadn't happened to him.

"'The same with that four billion dollars that America never paid the North,' Milner added. 'What – bow to that demand, just to get a few hundred Captain Clooneys back home? That wouldn't have been God-like at all, would it? So they never did – and here we are, forty years later.'"

****

"Looks like there's more. A lot of soldiers are appearing at the state capitols of Washington and Oregon," Ram said. "Militias are driving there cross-country. The Pentagon is getting into the act now too. The generals are saying that any man who shows up there is guilty of sedition."

"They're really serious about this!" Wanda cried.

"Better keep going, old man," I said to Paul, "and do it before we're all sent to the front lines. Besides, you're getting to the final act."

"I drove into Madrid with the men," Paul continued. "Nearly all of them had fallen asleep from the strong red wine. In the rear-view mirror, I could see McAnders murmuring to Rosetti, who was pushing tears out of his eyes. By then, I'd arranged things with him. He was going to buy a ticket for an overnight bus to the southern French city of Bayonne – this for the benefit of the security cameras – and then get in the boarding line for the bus but not quite get on. Then he would lay low for another hour till his bus for Medina del Campo left.

"I followed the GPS system through the tangles of ring roads surrounding Madrid and pulled up at Estación Sur, the city's main long-distance bus terminal. The men snapped awake, looking around confusedly. McAnders slid open the side door and grabbed his bag. In it were two hundred euros I'd given him and a bus ticket to Medina del Campo that the people in Casa Pepo had let me print out.

"'Headin' up to France, boys, place called Lourdes. They got this big ol' church where miracles happen. Gonna thank the Lord for gettin' us all outta 'Nam. Y'all watch out for Rosetti, hear?'

"'Will do,' called one guy at the back.

"'Good luck, Mark,' called another, starting a thunder of best wishes. Beside the door, Captain Clooney stuck out his hand: 'All the best, Corporal.'

"But what caught my eye was Dr. Milner, whose startled face was that of a man who had just realized that he had forgotten to turn off the stove burners at home. McAnders heaved the big door shut, and Milner opened his mouth, then stopped himself. That gave me a lot to think about as I drove the men into the center of the city to the house that had been prepared for them.

"It was a three-story stucco townhouse with an apple tree in the front yard. The Spanish Foreign Ministry used it for the staff of visiting dignitaries. Downstairs it had a living room, a dining room, and a big study with an oak desk and dreary shelves of Spanish legal tomes. In the kitchen a couple of cooks were preparing dinner. A Guardia Civil unit had been assigned to stand guard in their 4WD for the night.

"'We're a go, Paul,' Gormley told me by phone. 'Pentagon knows something's in the wind – Christ knows how – but they're just flailing around. The jet's ready and the crew will be on board bright and early tomorrow morning. We're looking at a ten a.m. wheels-up.'

"I stayed long enough to have dinner with the men – and to keep an eye on Milner. For some reason, that look of his when McAnder got off the bus just rubbed me the wrong way. It was like an affront to him, and he bitched to the others that they'd better not try the same thing: 'I go to all this trouble so a guy can go to *Lourdes?* Ask some god-damn statue for miracles? And all of you wishing him well! Dumbshits! I should have left you all in Hanoi!'

"So the atmosphere at dinner was pretty sub-dued, and afterwards nearly all the men went up to their rooms. Two ore three remained, watching CNN in the living room; they were agog watching a *black* president talking with reporters in the Oval Office – except Milner, who smirked at them. I went out to have a word with the Guardia Civil officers. I let drop that there were enemies in certain foreign governments who didn't want the Americans to depart tomorrow. That sharpened them a bit, and they called for extra cars to be posted at each end of the street, to check everyone in and out.

"But I kept an eye on the men through the window, and I saw Milner get up and leave the living room. I went in and found him in the study, hunched over, his back to the door as he talked on the desk telephone. He was speaking Vietnamese. And from the riffs of slashed syllables I picked out 'McAnder' and 'Lourdes.' It was a tense conversation, and Milner ended it with a growl as he snapped off the phone. Then he saw me.

"'Hell's your problem, Klippen? Your mother never taught you to knock?'

"'Yes, but she said that if I caught someone in an act of betrayal, I could go right in. So *you're* our Judas, huh? Awful lot of trouble to go to just to mess up your own plan.'

"Milner pulled a hand over his little beard a few times and then leaned back in the chair, as if he didn't give a hoot; I don't think there was much he ever *did* give a hoot about. 'The plan got messed up in the Mediterranean. I figured the V'etnamese would eventually trace our ship out of Haiphong, but with our transfer in Gwadar we'd give them the slip – at least long enough to make Newark. I never thought they'd contact the Americans; Hanoi's never admitted it held back prisoners. But foreign policy makes strange bedfellows, doesn't it?'

"'I've been a diplomat long enough to know.'

"'The P.O.W. thing is as big an embarrassment to one side as to the other: the V'etnamese don't need the scandal of a bunch of guys showing up on American TV saying they were held as P.O.W.s forty years after the war. And the Pentagon doesn't want to admit they covered up our existence.'

"'Assuming the story gets out to the public,' I said drily.

"'When I heard the Americans were on to us, I knew the jig was up. So I had to improvise: play both sides against the middle. Since that first town you took us to on the coast, I've been in contact with 'Nam, and I've made it clear to them that it's *the men* who kidnapped *me*. And with these reports, I've reinforced the message.'

"'But don't you want to go back to the States?' I asked.

"Milner looked around the room – the book shelves, the elegant floor lamps, the tall french windows – as if they held the answer. Finally, he shrugged. 'Might be fun, but I really don't give a damn either way. The University of Canberra will support me. We're working on two breakthrough projects on pancreatic cancer: Nobel Prize-level stuff that started with some berries I saw country doctors using in the jungle.'

"'The country doctors: I remember you mentioning them.'

"'That was the whole idea behind my putting together the escape from V'etnam. I need to go to Australia for conferences, and the scientists there are getting suspicious about why I can't; never told them I was a prisoner. Now that the escape's gone sideways, I figure I'll have finally earned my stripes: the V'etnamese will let me travel alone – to Australia or medical congresses in Singapore and the like – without worrying that I won't come back.'

"'And to hell with the other men.'

"Milner scowled at me as if he were condemned to talk to an idiot. 'I've been a prisoner for forty years, Mr. Klippen, I'll do as I damn well please.'

"'Sounds a bit God-like, actually.'

"'Why not?' he said with that twisted grin. 'I'm a surgeon, you know: I've always liked playing God.'

"'Well, I just talked with the CIA – they're handling this. They tell me everything is set for tomorrow. So it looks like you won't have to worry about the Vietnamese anymore.'

"He shrugged, glanced at a clock on the wall, stood up, yawned, and stretched his rail-thin frame. He wore a cloth belt that hung low across his hips. 'Maybe. Maybe. Believe it when I see it. Like I say, it's all the same to me, but....' He gestured at the phone. 'Don't underestimate the V'etnamese, Klippen. We did that in the war, and it ended badly.'"

****

By now, on the other side of the continent, the drama was deepening. The Oregon National Guard was digging in, and U.S. Army troops were entering the area, though many of the latter were refusing to fire on fellow Americans. The Pentagon generals were livid. "The president is in a meeting with the Joint Chiefs," Ram reported gloomily. "Well, guys, I tried to make the best of a bad situation. But...looks like the Oregon National Guard is going to ruin my party."

We all protested, telling Ram it had been a great party.

"Paul, at least tell us the end of the story," he said.

"Yeah. What happened, Paul?" asked Wanda. "Did the guys get to tell their story to anyone?"

"I never heard a word about this on the news," said Cindy. "They must have handled it pretty quietly."

"What happened?" Paul repeated, looking into his glass. "Dear god." He rattled the single ice cube still in it, and to me there's no more melancholy sound except the cry of a beggar. Cindy offered to get him a refill, but he just shook his head. "I'm almost done anyway." He looked up at the reddish night sky, silent.

"Want me to tell the story, old man?" I offered gently.

"No. I still have to do penance, and this is part of it."

He took a breath. "I got to the house early next morning and found that in addition to the Guardia Civil units, four rough-looking American guys in Army-green pants and black T-shirts were hanging around outside the entrance. They had biceps like footballs and looked as if they were ready to run an obstacle course. Surely these were the gorillas that the Pentagon had sent a few days earlier. They weren't armed or anything, but with bodies like those they didn't need to be. I had shown my i.d. to the Guardia Civil at the end of the street, and the ones in front of the gate nodded me through. But now one of the gorillas stepped up and asked me who I was. I told him and said I was from the embassy. This seemed to puzzle the men.

"'You aren't the one coming from Washington?'

"'No. I'm from the embassy,' I repeated. 'Is someone coming from Washington?'

"'I.d.,' the man said, holding out his hand. You know the type: eyes flat as a cliff of slate.

"'How about showing me yours? *I'm* in charge of the men here.'

"This brought skeptical smirks amongst the others. The man hesitated a moment, then pulled his passport out of his back pocket.

"'I know your nationality. What I'd like to see is your i.d.'

"'We were assigned here this morning,' said one of the others.

"'Assigned by who?'

"The man figured they'd answered enough questions from a mere civilian. 'Just assigned.'

"I let a beat pass. 'All right, assigned to do what?'

"'Keep things under control. Make sure our servicemen get on the bus okay. You got a problem with that, sir?'

"Well, such is the way of our military men. 'I'm sure that'll be very helpful,' I said, and walked past them.

"The men were eating a breakfast of rolls, cheese, and cold cuts, and a tangled 'Good morning' rose from them.

"'Hey, Pau'. You eat somethin', okay?' It was little Rosetti, who hopped off his chair and guided me to the table by the sleeve.

"'Well, Rosetti, it seems your English is finally coming back. Congratulations.'

"'Yah, got more Englich now. Gonna need some, you know?'

"I sat down and had a cup of coffee and a roll. The men were all wearing new warm-up suits, dark-blue, with stripes down the sides. They had arrived that night, as Gormley's plan had called for.

"'They tell us the bus will come by in about ten minutes,' Milner said. He motioned with his head at the gorillas outside. 'Those guys showed up this morning. I guess they're supposed to make sure everything goes smoothly.' He seemed disappointed, and I have to admit I felt a bit smug.

"I was finishing my coffee when a pale little priest of a man came fussing through the door. I groaned: Dale Ackerman, one of those State Department eternals who seemed to make himself useful to any administration that happened to have been elected. He didn't age really, just turn an ashier shade of mauve with the years: same lifeless mauve hair combed over a mostly bald head, same mauve tie, same disgracefully scuffed mauve shoes and bothered air of a man doing the bidding of kings. The only difference I noticed was that he had a two-day patina of beard stubble. I got up and said hello.

"'Paul. Hi. Flew in this morning straight out of a meeting at State. Okay, ah... come with me. Is there some place we can....'

"I led him to the study. He closed the door behind us.

"'I've been on the phone all night flying here, but I think, ah, we're, ah, all set. The Spanish Air Force has a C-130 transport with crew ready. It was the only option available at short notice. Major consequence here: this has to be handled carefully. We don't want the Spaniards, ah, *discommoded* in any way.'

"'Not the CIA jet? The men will be disappointed,' I said with as straight a face as I could. You always found yourself doing that with Ackerman, he was so ridiculously grave.

"'No. CIA has been, ah, dealt out of the table. What else? The plane is being provisioned with a lot of American fast food. We thought that would be a nice touch. We got a McDonald's restaurant out of bed to make rations, and a pizza place too. We think that will make up for the, ah, less-than-optimal conditions. But it was the C-130 or nothing: L-shaped seat bolted to the sides, not all that warm. We're hoping to get in a cot or two and some blankets. There are toilet facilities, a microwave and a coffee maker. If we have time we'll get in a couple of magazines. It's, ah, not going to be all that fun, I'm afraid.'

"'Well, it's only seven hours or so, how bad can it be?' I said. 'Besides, these are pretty tough guys, even though they're –'

"Ackerman's head bobbed up at me. 'Seven? I was told it was twelve to fourteen.'

"'My god, where are they flying them to? Pearl Harbor?'

"'No, Hanoi.'

"'*Hanoi?* The men are going back to *Hanoi?*'

"'Well, we certainly can't fly them to the States.'

"I must have stood like stone so long that Ackerman gave up waiting for me to say something.

"'It has been felt, in Washington, Paul, that our relationship with the Government of Vietnam would be, ah, *seriously impaired* by the...ah, well, if it *emerged* that these men had been held prisoner there for so long. Furthermore, the DoD has weighed in and said that these men could not possibly be the, ah, the men they claim to be. But their mere presence and *claims* of being P.O.W.s would be cause for a serious –'

"'They *are* who they claim to be!' I hissed. 'One of them can barely speak English anymore. The Pentagon certainly believed them enough to blow their ship out of the water.'

"'That's a matter beyond my pay-grade, Paul. The Vietnamese, furthermore –'

"'And *fuck* the Vietnamese! Forty years they've kept these men – their whole lives! They're in their seventies and they just want to go back to their own country again. Some of those guys spent years living in caves! And you're going to send them *back* to that?'

"'Paul, Paul, Paul – please. This is no time to get emotional. The Vietnamese have assured us that the men will not be, ah, ill-treated when they return. One of them is an eminent doctor, for example, and he will return to his work. The rest will be furloughed and, ah, basically retired.'

"I laughed in his face. 'And you believe that?'

"'We have their assurance.'

"'Dale, the last *assurance* the Vietnamese gave us was that they wouldn't invade the south again. Maybe this time we'd better err on the side of –'

"He interrupted me. 'Paul, this is a bigger-picture issue, okay? The Vietnamese have, ah, *expressed* to us that they are trying extremely hard to walk a tightrope between good relations with us and also with China, which is building one shoe factory after another in their country. It is definitely *not* the moment to give Hanoi a reason to move-into-*slash*-lean-towards China's orbit. China is slowly neutralizing everyone on its borders, and Vietnam, because of the long-standing bad blood between them and the Chinese, is a valuable asset. It would be extremely unwise on our part to be doing anything to damage their, their, ah, *balance* on said tightrope.'"

Paul clacked the ice around his glass again: that lonely sound. "By the time he'd finished, I understood why the gorillas were outside and why the CIA had been 'dealt out.'

"'But the men don't know about the change of plans, do they?' I said.

"'It has been felt, Paul, that this is the easiest way to handle the situation without, as I've implied, *discommoding* the Spaniards – who have really stepped up nicely to this thing, you know, supplying facilities and a crew so quickly. The clearest course right now would be to, ah, wish the men a pleasant flight and let them come to grips with new, ah, ah, *calibrations* once the ramp is lowered in Hanoi.'"

Paul looked around at us. "This on an airplane, you understand, that doesn't have any windows. And at the moment of truth, the pilots could stay locked in their cabin. I took a deep breath and said, 'And I suppose *it has been felt in Washington* that someone is supposed to inform them of the change in airplanes and the length of the flight and so on. After all, the men think they're flying seven hours to Langley.'

"'The point is not to discommode –'

"'Discommode the Spaniards, right,' I finished. 'Or give the strong-arm boys out there any reason to send them back with their hands 'cuffed behind their backs and hoods over their heads. I get it, I get it.' And now I remembered a black duffle bag lying on the steps of the house. Surely that was where the cuffs and hoods were stored.

"Ackerman gave me a mannish whack on the shoulder – probably something he had learned to do in one of those leadership training courses. 'We know we can count on you, Paul. Your record in Washington is excellent.' Meaning, of course, that it *wouldn't* be excellent if I balked.

"I heard a cheer go up from the dining room. The bus had arrived to pick up the men. Without a word to Ackerman, I walked out."

Paul stared at the table. "In the fifteen feet that I walked down the hallway, I think I aged twenty years. It's a good thing that the men had all gone upstairs to collect their things because it took me some moments to compose my face. But finally the men assembled in the foyer, me with my back to the front door. Milner was at the far end of the group, a quizzical look on his face. And some steps behind him was mauve little Ackerman with a cell phone pressed to his ear.

"'Okay, guys, before you leave, there are a couple of changes that have been made that I need to tell you about,' I began. For some reason I was rubbing my hands together as if they were cold; I didn't know what to do with them. 'First, well, there's some bad news. At the end, you're not going in a cool 12-seater CIA jet with a cute flight attendant to serve you whiskey. But there *will be* some whiskey on the flight, isn't that right, Mr. Ackerman?' I pointed over the men's heads. 'Dale Ackerman, from the State Department, guys. He's doing last-minute details.'

"The men turned and rumbled a greeting. 'T'anks, Mist' Ack'man,' chirped little Rosetti.

"'You bet, Paul. We'll, ah, we'll get a bottle on board.' His ear was still to his phone.

"'Great. Ah, the other thing is,' I continued, 'the plane is a big C-130 transport that the Spanish Air Force has provided, and it's not too comfortable: seats bolted to the sides, you know.'

"'At least we'll be able to walk around a bit, stretch our legs,' said another man, and the rest cheered again.

"'That is the upside, for sure,' I said. 'The only thing is that the flight's not going to be seven hours. It's going to be about twelve or thirteen hours in the air. I guess they're flying you to a base in ah... ah....' Suddenly, I couldn't think of a base that was twelve hours away.

"'San Diego,' Ackerman put in. 'Camp Pendleton. It was thought that the facilities there for physical exams and reinsertion into society were well-suited to –'

"'Aw, Pendleton? With a lot of fuckin' *Marines?*' griped Captain Clooney, turning around to him. Remember he was a Navy man? 'How about the 32nd Street Naval Base on the coast? Pendleton's airstrip's shit: out in the fuckin' desert!'

"'We didn't know you had a preference,' said Ackerman smoothly. 'Consider it done: 32nd Street it is.'

"'Okay! Listen, guys, greatest place in the world,' Clooney told the others. 'They got a pool club. Open all year round. Restaurants. At least when *I* was there. And you can...'

"He went on, describing the wonders of the base, and Milner caught my eye. Hand pressed to his mouth, he was laughing uncontrollably, his torso waving back and forth like a branch in the wind. He knew what was going on. Just to spite him, I wanted to blurt, *This is all a lie! They're taking you back to Vietnam! Run, guys, run for it! Smack those killers at the entrance and run for it! They can't get you all!*

"But of course I didn't. I only told the men that a big load of good ol' American fast food was being loaded on board as we spoke, and there would be a few cots for guys to lie down on."

Paul was silent, running a finger around the rim of his empty glass: around and around. "They cheered me. They thanked me, shook my hand one by one as they went out the door. Rosetti threw his arms around me and kissed my chest. Barely keeping a poker face, Milner passed without a word or a glance. Onto the bus they marched, and at the end of the street, the Guardias Civiles waved back to the roaring men as the bus passed. Then they were gone. Three days later, the C-130 returned to Spain and I drafted a statement for the ambassador thanking the Spanish Defense Ministry for its cooperation, which symbolized the smooth relations between the Kingdom of Spain and the United States of America."

****

As we were gathering at Ram's front door, purses recovered, car keys jangling, cell phones clucking into life again, I said, "Hold on, Paul. What about McAnder? Never bloody well asked you about him. Whatever happened to him?"

"Yeah, he sounded like a pretty nice guy," said Cindy.

"McAnder. Right. I was hoping you'd forget about him." Paul was pulling on a light jacket. He looked down at the floor as if gathering his strength, and he swallowed noisily. "Let's see. My posting to Embassy Madrid ended about a year later...call it fifteen months. There was a search for him, I know that. Craig Gormley kept me informed for several weeks, but he was called back to Langley, where I heard they put him in charge of counting staples for the secretarial pool. He had taken full credit for the matter, and when things fell apart, so did his career.

"I was questioned twice by different agencies about McAnder, and you can never be too sure about those guys and their devious methods. So I was reluctant to go up to that monastery and say hello. Instead, on our last weekend in Spain, Cindy and I drove down to Urda, strolled around a bit, and stopped in at the big church there. I left Cindy to wander around inside and talked to Padre Diego in his office.

"'Brother Mark, yes, he was very happy at the monastery,' he told me in Spanish. 'He fixed many things for the monks, and his Spanish was getting better. But about two months ago, he disappeared. He went to the nearby city, Medina del Campo, to go to the hospital there. The Church had arranged to get him a public-health insurance card, you know, and organized his visa for him. The Church can still get a few delicate things done in this country,' he added proudly.

"'And McAnder disappeared?' I said.

"'Not two weeks after getting his papers straightened out. He went to the hospital for his appointment. Brother Miguel drove him and did some shopping for the monastery while Brother Mark was with the doctor. The poor man had hurt his back in the monastery. He was such a hard worker – and so happy! Up with the sun every day, cooking meals for everyone, sweeping the chapel, studying his Spanish....' He flapped his arms uselessly.

"'And he vanished. It seems Brother Mark never even entered the hospital. Brother Miguel had stopped across the street and pointed out the entrance, and that was the last anyone saw of the poor man. Miguel called the Guardia Civil, asked all over – they even called me, just in case Brother Mark had come to Urda. Nothing. So strange. But there was something a bit strange about Brother Mark: something in his past.'

"'What was that?' I asked.

"'He never said exactly, just that – I'm not sure how to say this. When he arrived at the monastery, Brother Miguel wanted to get a residence visa for him. But Brother Mark told him to wait. He made Brother Miguel wait several more months before beginning the process. Brother Mark said he wanted some kind of trouble to blow over first. He didn't say what kind it was.' He shook his head. 'They said a Mass for him just last week, and I said another one here. A fine man, a good man. I cannot understand what kind of trouble such a person could get into.'"

Paul took off his glasses and pinched the tears out of his eyes. "And that's what happened to McAnder," he whispered.

We said good-night to Ram and went to our cars. Off in the distance we heard the rending growl of an explosion: the creak of history. Without a word, we drove off on our separate ways.

Author's Afterword:
I've stayed true to the facts regarding the history of American P.O.W.s left in Vietnam after the war, and about Robert Garwood. There are a lot of good resources regarding this extraordinarily sad story. Here are some that I found helpful.
Kiss the Boys Goodbye: How the United States betrayed its own POWs in Vietnam (Skyhorse; 2014), by Monika Jensen-Stevenson and William Stevenson, *reviews the entire issue, including their friendship with the recently-returned Garwood, and profiles her fight to get a segment about the issue on* 60 Minutes, *where she worked as a producer.*
An Enormous Crime: The Definitive Account of American POWs abandoned in Southeast Asia

(Thomas Dunne Books; 2008), by Bill Hendon and Elizabeth A. Stewart, *lives up to its boast of "definitive," detailing North Vietnamese intentions to keep as many P.O.W.s as possible in order to ensure American compliance with war reparations. Hendon, a U.S. Congressman from North Carolina, describes his clashes with State Department bigwigs like Richard Armitage, who told him flatly: "Look, Congressman, it's over. These men serve at the pleasure of their commander-in-chief, and when he decides it's time for them to come home, they'll come home."*

The Men We Left Behind: Henry Kissinger, the Politics of Defeat and the Tragic Fate of POWs after the Vietnam War, by Mark A. Sauter and James D. Sanders *(National Press Books; 2018). This book has a particularly interesting section on how American P.O.W.s were moved to other countries to be used as laborers, and perhaps even as guinea pigs for experiments.*

Expendable: Abandoned POWs in Vietnam. *Robert Garwood, with humor and humanity, tells his full story in this video available on YouTube.*

John McCain and the POW Cover-Up *is one of several articles by New York Times reporter Sydney Schanberg. None of the major newspaper and magazines, however, would publish his accounts on abandoned prisoners of war, which goes to show how the media conspires in the cover-up. His articles are easy to find on Unz.com and TheAmericanConservative.com. This article in particular details the evidence of P.O.W.s left in Vietnam and the role of Senator John McCain in covering up their existence.*

THE RAINMAKER

(based on the true facts of an untrue story)

Author's note:

The 2011 American raid on Osama bin Laden's enormous house in Abbottabad, Pakistan, was surely a fake, intended to close out the matter of bin Laden, the alleged director of the attacks of September 11, 2001, and also to promote the re-election of President Barack Obama in the following year. Bin Laden, incidentally, denied any involvement in 9-11 twice before the month of September was out, and post-2001 videos of bin Laden taking credit for the attacks are widely considered false; the bin Ladens in the videos are clearly other men, as is the blurry video of bin Laden miraculously discovered by American forces in the initial weeks of the invasion of Afghanistan. In it, a false, and rather chubby, bin Laden cheerfully discusses the attacks with other men at some type of social function, perhaps a wedding.

People who have studied bin Laden say that he most likely died at the end of 2001; and due to his acute kidney problems he could not possibly have survived until the raid by Navy Seals in May 2011. The inspiration for the following story/satire is the widely-reported fact that the CIA, which had the bin Laden compound under surveillance for six months before the raid, told President Obama just two days before it that they could not guarantee that bin Laden was there. This aspect of the raid legend has always seemed to me improbable. Can it possibly be true that the CIA, which is not exactly a gum-shoe detective agency, could not detect one man in one house over a period of six months? Hence the following satire: my deconstruction of the narrative told to the public. The words in boldface refer to real facts of the event.

THE RAINMAKER HAD WORKED – he disdained the term "served" – as a government employee for forty-seven years, and had never lost his raw wonder at the blockheads, both the wide- and narrow-eyed, who played the World's Great Game. To stay awake in the meeting, he resorted to his usual trick: with one hand, he took apart and reassembled a pen – unscrewed the middle, pulled out the cartridge, pulled off its spring, held all four components parallel and flat in his palm, then put it all back together again. He was not ambidextrous, but after decades of long moaning meetings, he could do this with either hand, and so fast that anyone would gasp in amazement if they saw it — but he did it under the table.

That's it, children, argue yourselves out, he silently told the scrapping officials. *Then you'll be ready for the Voice of Reason.* It was what he called his Meeting Rope-a-Dope. And did these people ever need his Voice – Chip Bookbinder had that one right on the money.

Why? Because the hard-boiled CIA guy up front by the screen, laser pointer in hand, was telling the truth and wasn't budging from his position. This vexed the many top officials assembled – NSA, White House, State, Pentagon, and sundry emissaries from the far-flung empire of American security – vexed them just on general principles: in Washington, telling the actual rank truth only showed weakness. And as to budging from a position, well, we all budged eventually. It was just a question of more access, control, or budget. All of which had been offered – graciously, frankly, generously – and *still* the CIA guy was sticking to his point like a barnacle to a hull.

That is: here they were, end of April, just days away from the scheduled raid on Osama bin Laden's house in Abbottabad, Pakistan – wavelengths assigned, teams limbered up, choppers gassed — and CIA was tossing a stick into the churning spokes of America's War on Terror.

Following White House orders, CIA, dubious yet dutiful, **had trailed Osama bin Laden's personal courier** right to The Man's huge house in Abbottabad – all this the **previous September. CIA discreetly set up surveillance** of the house. Cameras in the guise of chunks of cement, arms busted off little dolls, and used condoms gazed without blinking at those four mammoth walls day after day. Listening gadgets beamed microwaves – from down the street, from across the rooftops, from a hundred miles up in the cold dentist's waiting room of space – beamed them so long and hard that, as the CIA guy put it, "everyone in the goddamn place should have been turned into roast beef by now."

Yet **not a voice-printable peep** was heard from Osama – not so much as an "Anybody seen where I left my glasses?"

Nor had a single glimpse of his six-foot-six frame lumbering past the windows been wrung from the terabytes of video streamed 24/7 week after monotonous week.

Could The Man be *that* security conscious? After all, the compound's inhabitants **burned their own trash** rather than have it trucked away, lest some street urchin come across The Man's fingerprints on a Pakistani *Playboy*. **The kids shepherded to school each morning** never once let slip to classmates anything about Grandpa Osama, causing the White House rep to mutter, "Wish I had staff that reliable." And as bad luck would have it, there was **no phone line to tap**, though surely the neighbors – neighbors being neighbors the world over – all wondered why someone would build **two million dollars** of bad taste on their street and not put in a phone line.

"And that has led to our considered conclusion," the CIA man had said, winding up his 45-minute presentation, "that Subject bin Laden is not there and never was. The courier – if he was a courier at all — was someone else's."

The room was stunned. The room raised holy hell.

For two hours.

"What kinda bullshit is this, boy?" an Air Force general roared, quiet until then. "All the time in the world, finest e-lint money can buy, and you boys can't find one man in one house?"

"Yes! Exactly! Right! Hallelujah, it's finally sinking in!" the CIA guy cried in exasperation, tie now pulled down to his second button. "Because he's not there. Get it, folks? The reason we don't see him or hear him is – watching the lips this time, right? – *he is not there.* End of story."

For the first time in two hours, silence writhed down the lovely oaken table — a long one, supporting the cufflinks and purses of twelve Type-A bureaucrats.

Except at the far end of it, where The Rainmaker sat in his worn black suit and wrinkled tie, one pylon-like elbow propped on the table, his crew-cut balanced on that. His hand worked furiously under the table — he could take apart and re-assemble his pen in twelve seconds — and even with that it was hard to stay awake.

Well, looks like we're finally getting worn down. Thank god! Five more minutes and I'm going to turn into rigor mortis.

Halfway up the table, the White House rep – in shirt sleeves like his boss, with whom that morning he'd played "a couple quick three-on-threes, it being such a nice spring day" — swatted back his chair and jumped to his feet.

"Now just wait a goddamn minute. What the hell is this?" he griped. "I've got a president looking at re-election in the middle of a recession, and he's not going to miss out on this. He's kissed the ass of every one of you guys from day one. Anybody here lacking for budget? Huh? Anybody worried about joining the legions of jobless? Anybody see anything less than a brilliant career path ahead straight through till retirement? Huh? C'mon, speak up if you do — now's the time."

Nobody spoke up.

And like the many presidential flunkies The Rainmaker had seen over five decades in government, this one even had his boss's gestures. He slowly put his hands on his hips to highlight for one and all the flatness of his abdomen.

Of course, that face is so bony you might not have eaten but a leaf of lettuce in six months, The Rainmaker mused.

"All right, all right, all right, so Osama's not there. Great. Okay. Fine. *Like I give a fuck!* Then you *make* him there. The Seals are ready to go. They've been **practicing on the mock-up house** for weeks. So you *make* him there."

The CIA man's face — and it was a big, loose, pale one under left-parted hair — was bright red. The Rainmaker read him as the kind of man who lost every argument with his wife; Chip had chosen him well. "No way. Not a chance. Not doing it, not going down that road again. The heavy boys go in and it turns out he's not there, and then it's *our* people explaining to the sub-committee why we were all wrong *again*. A repeat of the **Iraq debacle with WMD** *again*. Forget it. Besides, we told you guys from the get-go: the man kicked it of **kidney failure two months after the invasion.** He never saw 2002. A half-dozen **Mideast newspapers reported his death**, and practically every in-theater asset we had came back with the same thing. Did we tell you or did we not?"

"Did we approve your budgets hardly changing a comma, or did we not?" retorted the White House rep.

Why don't you just pull down your pants, see whose dick is bigger and get it over with? The Rainmaker wondered with a sigh.

The CIA man looked around at the unwilling faces; his opinion was not popular. "C'mon, people, he was **on double dialysis**, for Chrissakes. Nobody — repeat, *nobody* — could survive ten more years in that condition."

More writhing silence. The Rainmaker put away his pen, took a deep breath, and spoke.

"One man's opinion here, but..." he said in his viscous old Midwestern drawl, all heads turning his way. Of all those present, he was the only one without a title before his blotter. "It's all a question of narratives, isn't it? You're just using the wrong one."

"May I ask who you are and what your agency is?" snapped the White House man, tie wagging as he leaned over the table to get a look at the speaker.

"Oh, what's in a name? Chip Bookbinder asked me to step in. I keep an office down the hall from his. I'm just kind of coasting along till retirement, to be honest." Harrington Bookbinder was deputy director of the CIA. "People send me psy ops for critique and vetting." *And what hare-brained ops!* he despaired silently. "NSA, CIA, just about everybody. The team that polices 9-11 Truthers calls me when they're in a jam – that sort of thing."

At the mention of 9-11, several faces at the table went red.

"Now then," The Rainmaker went on, leaning back in his chair and propping an ankle on a knee. "The problem is not the facts on the ground, but the narrative you give them. CIA doesn't need to say bin Laden's not there. Just say, 'Well, there was just such-and-such a possibility that we'd find him there.'" He held up a hand before the objections started. "What kind of phrasing would we be looking at here? 'Possibility' needs weakening. Let me think..."

There was a skeptical chuckle to his right, and The Rainmaker turned his head that way and for a long moment nailed an Army Intel colonel in his gaze. The man fell silent. "If you are in the mood for humor, Colonel, I suggest you go inspect your troops."

"That was uncalled for, sir," the colonel mumbled.

The Rainmaker looked at his long pale hands, which he wrung for some seconds on his knee. "Ah! Yes, the correct phrase is, '**A *strong* possibility.**' That's the ticket."

"Strong or weak," huffed the CIA man. "What difference does it make?"

"Now let's roll the new narrative and hear how it sounds," The Rainmaker continued. He cleared his throat and let the silence gather. When he spoke, it was with a deepened voice and the patter of a news anchor:

"'As late as two days before the raid, the best the CIA could say was that there was a strong possibility that Osama bin Laden was in the mansion. They could tell the president that they were'" – The Rainmaker paused – "'**highly confident**. The president asked for confirmation but they could not give it. They gave certain odds, they made certain assumptions — that was the best they could do. Between a rock and a hard place, the president took a risk, gambling his presidency in the bargain. He gave the Seals the green light.'" He stopped and looked at the CIA man at the head of the table. "On board so far?"

"Depends," he said. "You go in, there's no Osama. Now what? Finish it."

The Rainmaker didn't – not for the moment – and looked at the White House rep still sprawled over the table. "And POTUS?"

"Yeah, yeah, sure. That'll play. Keep going."

"No. No, not quite," said The Rainmaker. "You'll need to divert attention from the fact that it's just a house and one man hasn't shown up inside it. So you'll want a lot of moaning and groaning about how hard the op was: Taliban spies everywhere, all the neighbors around, **military academy right down the road**. And just for good measure, for example, for example…Yes! You **red-teamed** it first. There we are. You brought in **another team of intelligence analysts and presented your findings to them. They agreed: he's there.** I can bring in my own staff this evening if you'd like, just for the verisimilitude: reserve the secure room, make a fuss, order in Chinese, walk out looking grave and statesmanlike."

The rest of the people were chuckling.

God, what children you are. It's like you're plotting to soap the neighbors' windows.

"Excuse me, sir," called a Marine general down the table. "I believe I've heard of you. Would you by any chance be the man known as The Rainmaker?"

A modest smile. "An old baseball nickname, I'm afraid, General."

More laughter. The Rainmaker dipped into his patience.

"Well then, the rest is merely decoration," he went on. "The Seals drop in, enter the house and… what? They find one of the men. This unlucky fellow is now our Osama. The Seals terminate him along with all other males — **leaving the children**

and females, whose account one way or the other will hold no weight in the Muslim world. They pack up the body with a lot of laptops and electronic files and then — "

"Hold on. Just hold it right there. That would never fly," said the CIA man. "That won't work at all. We're going to *take down* the man who is at the center of al Qaeda? Like fucking hell we are. We would haul him down to Gitmo and squeeze him like a tube of toothpaste till he coughed up every last detail of his networks. Everybody knows that, and if they don't, the *Times* is going to remind them the next day."

The Rainmaker could not quite hide his amusement. "Now of course, that's true. But when the president of the United States calls a surprise press conference and announces that we just put a bullet through Osama bin Laden's brain, well, I think good Americans will overlook the loss of intel." Suppressing a sigh, he again waited for the laughter to subside. "With all respect, you live in Langley, Virginia. The folks who need to hear the narrative live in Memphis and Palo Alto and Dayton."

The CIA man puffed out his cheeks, shrugged, and finally said, "All right, I'll stretch a point – fine. But then what about the body? You just *killed* a guy calling him Osama bin Laden. You can't leave the guy there for anyone to discover. But how do you justify **weighing down a chopper** all the way back to Bagram Air Base?"

"Yeah, that's right," said the White House rep nervously.

The Rainmaker had an ugly lower-teeth-only smile like a line of gray tenements, which he now displayed. "To check his DNA, of course."

"We *have* his DNA."

"Exactly. And now **we check his DNA against the sample** that we have. To i.d. him."

The CIA guy stared as if talking to an idiot. "You kill him and *then* you check his DNA?"

"You would rather that we checked it before?"

Everyone chuckled.

What I wouldn't give to take a photo of you all, The Rainmaker thought. *The Gadarene swine could have not posed more beautifully before running over the cliff.*

"I think the point is, son, to have an excuse to get the guy outta there," said the Air Force general to the CIA man.

The CIA guy could see he wasn't going to win this battle either. "All right, I'll buy it — *for now,*" he pouted.

"Okay. Now we have a body and we are ready to go," said The Rainmaker. "The **Seals pack everything up with a lot of laptops and hard drives and pendrives** soon to be used to complete our narrative – and let's not ponder too deeply the fact that bin Laden never struck anyone as a computer wonk. Off we fly to Bagram. At first light, **the Pakistani police swoop in and carry off the women and children**. There *is* a **long-standing agree-**

ment, I believe, between CIA and the Paki ISI regarding bin Laden?"

The CIA man rolled his eyes as if to concede a single point. "Yes, **we have full rights on capture in Pakistan** if we locate bin Laden there. I would *imagine* they'll cooperate."

"All the same, you'll want them to **raise Caine for the violation of their sacred territory**. Everyone: ISI, Congress, Musharraf, Paki media, president, the works."

"They won't need much encouragement," the CIA man said drily.

"Indeed – but key for the verisimilitude. And for the sake of narrative, we'll need some color. For example..." The Rainmaker wrung his hands twice. "The Seals burst in **just as bin Laden was reaching for an AK-47** leaning against the wall. And let's bring in a woman – that always adds the right dabs of blues and violets. Yes, **let's say a woman – a bin Laden wife, say — stepped in front of Osama**, who wasn't gentleman enough to object. And let's say **someone tried to defend him, maybe a son** – all in the fanatical spirit of defending the great man to the death. Whatever – the details needn't connect."

See? Even you are hypnotized. The moment you enter the story, you're helpless, The Rainmaker observed, pausing for someone who sneezed.

"Actually, the more blurry the raid is, the better," he went on. "Let **one version come out, then another, then another**. Let the public pick and choose. Nothing stinks more to high hell than the classic seamless narrative."

"Wow! I get the feeling you've done this before," the White House rep joked.

"C'mon – finish it. What about the body?" snapped the CIA guy.

"Simple. **Once back at Bagram, Forensics checks out the body**, takes photos, does the DNA, and then...Well, I suppose you couldn't just bury him – that would be sticking a hand into the hornet nest. Better to cremate him after a moving religious ceremony presided over by an Army Muslim cleric because we...No – no, that's madness. The bin Laden family would ask for a box of ashes, wouldn't they? As would half the Muslim world. No, you...where could you....Ah! **You fly the body directly out to a waiting aircraft carrier**. Moving **Islamic ceremony**, the body **dropped into the sea**." A frown. "No. You would want to be *very* careful with the verb there: 'lowered,' 'slid,' or 'condemned to the sea.' Isn't that what the sailors do?"

"I believe the phrase you're looking for, sir, is 'committed to the deep,'" said a Navy Intel man politely.

"Thank you, Captain. Yes, 'committed to the deep.' And as to the media, 'lowered,' 'slid,' or, or... **'eased into the sea.'** Yes, that's our ticket: 'eased.' Because we're a feeling people, even with our bitterest enemies. We're above them. Even bin Laden gets his final ashes-to-ashes with a few bowed heads by his side." The Rainmaker looked around. "Everyone happy?"

Silence, which no longer writhed, but slithered.

"This is great stuff," said the White House man. "Great stuff. Hell, you've got to come work on our re-election campaign! Are you available on any kind of — "

"And lastly we'll need the endgame," The Rainmaker went on hastily, to a few laughs. He stopped, looking up at the ceiling, one hand raised tensely. "No. Actually, in this case – public psy op, narrative built from the ground up...No, here you would do well to have **three endgames**, one for the immediate narrative, another a week or so later to reinforce, and another for the longer term, after the truthers have had their go at it. It won't take them long to tear into this, you know."

"Fuck 'em," said the CIA guy. "We should lock every one of those shits up and waterboard them till they're sponges."

"A truly counterproductive act," said The Rainmaker, and he needed a sharp effort not to add "you fool."

"How you figure?"

The Rainmaker addressed the table. "We *need* truthers, dear ones. We need them making their angry YouTube videos and blogs full of bad grammar and clichéd claptrap: 'blatant,' 'obvious,' 'utterly.' They are precisely the ones that make us look as if we have freedom of expression. What embarrassing bits they expose are pinpricks. Yes,

Internet is our *ally* – never forget that. We need practice no censorship at all because Internet does it for us: it turns everything into nothing. It churns truth and falsehood together in a way I could only have dreamed of years ago when I was briefing reporters in 'Nam."

The Rainmaker felt their astonishment pulse around the table. *Why does anyone need to explain this to you? Because you've never once lifted your faces out of a cell phone to think, that's why.*

After a silence, the White House rep said, "You said three endgames. What's the first one?"

"The first, well... You'll need to **release some kind of video** — like the one from **Jalalabad where bin Laden confessed to 9-11** at the wedding party? That was one of *my* jobs, by the way."

"Yeah, and that was a bang-up job if I ever saw it," sneered the CIA man, finally scoring a point. "9-11 Truthers cut that to ribbons."

"Yes, well, I apologize for my **fat bin Laden**. You know how it is: orders came down, not in the original plan, best we could do on short notice. Our model spent three hours in makeup, and even that and ten generations of video copying couldn't do much. But at least the **proper impression was made at the right time**, and that's the name of the game. The Truthers arrived far too late. Now then: let's think of another video, which will be released, say, forty-eight hours after the raid – first video from the stash that the Seals pick up. It should prove **bin Laden was recently alive**, and we would do well to imply that he still had **some type of organization supporting him**."

"How about bin Laden giving a speech to his people in the middle of the compound?" said a heavy, prim woman with a chain of pearls across her chest and the mysterious initials "ARR and J" before her blotter.

"Yes, not bad," said The Rainmaker. "And that would give us the extra plus of extended jihad after bin Laden dies." He tipped his head to either side. "But that would also involve an extended frontal view of him, and then we run into identification issues again. We really must avoid that this time. And then there's the background inside the compound. We have no idea what it looks like. We don't want anyone sneaking in there after the raid comparing our video with the cracks in the walls. No, we'll do best to keep it to **an enclosed room with an absolutely plain background**. And anything in it would **have to be moveable**. Stolen by the crowd long before the video hits the airwaves."

The ARR and J woman wasn't going to give up. "He could harangue people in a closed space in the house, and you could keep the camera behind him, trained mainly on the followers." She grinned suddenly at the others. "Hey, this is kinda fun."

"Uh-huh – better."

"He could have a Pakistani newspaper from last week in his hand," the man from the DIA tossed out. "We could have one flown over tomorrow."

"Yes, but you would run into the problem of specifying exactly what day it was. Not good. Ambiguity, dear ones, is always our ally."

For ten minutes, everyone contributed ideas and The Rainmaker fielded them, rejecting, honing, approving, modifying. *You're like a lot of happy college freshmen in a bull session. 'This is government at its finest!' you're thinking. My god, you belong in a Doonesbury comic strip.*

At the end, he said, "All right, I think we've got it: **a from-behind quartering shot of Osama** in a bare room, **a computer screen to one side**. He's watching a **video composite of news items** put together by his team. It should **show President Obama**, a few current events around the Middle East — **the Arab Spring** and so on. Can you put that together?" he asked the CIA man.

"I guess," he said skeptically. "But hell, it's going to look pretty damn convenient, isn't it? A video of him taken from behind so that you don't see his face very much? And what's on the screen just *happens* to be events that prove the vid's recent? A little obvious if you ask me."

The Rainmaker conceded this with a shrug.

"Besides, if you take video of somebody, what do you shoot?" the CIA man went on. "The guy playing with his grandchildren or – well, this is Islam – the guy praying on his rug. Whatever – the guy *doing* something. You're talking about a guy sitting on the floor watching TV, and your view is of his back? Who shoots vid of that?"

"Yes, yes, of course – point taken," The Rainmaker huffed. "But you're giving your fellow citizens far too much credit. All of these objections will pop up on leftist websites, but only among people who think outside of the box, which is very few." He was wringing his hands again. "Ah, may I ask a favor at this point?"

The CIA man flapped his elbows hopelessly. "Have I ever told you no?"

"When you shoot the scene, would you use a **skinny little hard-to-use remote control** and tell your model to hold it in his **right hand**?"

"Bin Laden is **left-handed**," the White House man put in impressively.

"*Was,*" snapped the CIA guy.

"Whatever," said The Rainmaker. "You see, in the Jalalabad video the Truthers caught me out on that one. I had our Osama filmed writing a note and **the pen was in his right hand**. It simply slipped my mind. I'd just like to give the Truthers a little jab so they know that I don't really give a pig's pod about their detective work. Do you mind?"

A shrug. "You got it – right hand it is."

"Thank you. Now then, the mid-range endgame. **Bits and bobs from the laptops** and pendrives should slowly come out – most of it very hush-hush, TS/TCI, but **pornography should figure prominently** – nothing dirties an image faster. And you'll want someone to mention **hair dye found in the house** – Grecian Formula, Just for Men, whatever. Vanity deflates the image too, and our latter Osamas over the years were indeed **a bit on the youthful side**."

"What about pictures, visuals?" said the White House rep. "If there aren't photos, people think it didn't happen."

The Rainmaker nodded. "Though for the life of me, I don't know why; the camera always lies."

That got a huge laugh.

The Rainmaker took out his pen, held it under the table, and went through his little drill, just to keep from shouting at them. *Because you still believe the camera, don't you, you fools? A whole lifetime of movies and TV news has made you as gullible as children before the puppet show.*

"But I think, in this case..." he went on at last. "Really, the best we can do is the *impression* of photos of bin Laden, the *news* of photos, rather than the photos themselves. Photo-shopping some old photos is but the work of an hour, and then we release them on a limited, official basis. We send — "

"Forget it," said the CIA man flatly. "The Truthers will go through ten thousand photos of bin Laden till they find the one we used."

"I said release them on a *limited, official* basis," The Rainmaker said patiently. "You **circulate them among White House staff, Secretary of State Clinton**, perhaps to the top level of DoD, everyone mulling and weighing and splitting hairs and debating like real adults: **to release or not to release?** That is the question. Because these photos are grotesque. Gory. One of the president's staffers spent fifteen minutes in the Oval Office bathroom puking his guts out after seeing them. And I think we can count on these good people not to check if the pictures are just photo-shopped old photos of Osama."

"Sure. Hey, we're on board, count on it," said the White House rep.

"And at the end?" The Rainmaker asked. "As one these sensitive elites shout no. The photos are just too awful to be released. Osama with his brains hanging out one ear. Osama missing a nose. **Osama with half his face blown off**. Decency-in-media associations would protest if we released them. Local PTAs. The AARP. The Pentagon should also weigh in: these photos would **play right into the propaganda hands** of our enemies. And the **solemn determination** is made: these photos will not come to light till well after The Second Coming."

"Well now, I don't know here," said the Marine general. You don't release any photos, sir, and you're not going to convince your grandmother. With all respect."

Others nodded vigorously. The Rainmaker wondered if any of them had greater intellect than the chairs they sat on. He pressed professorial fingertips together. "Let's remember, dear ones, that our job is not to convince, but merely to give people one or two good reasons *not to believe any other version*. This is a distinction that I'm always having to explain to various agencies. Sometimes, as in an espionage op, you certainly do need to convince.

But this is a public psy op. Here we play with a natural advantage" – a tiny chuckle – "and I would imagine it drives the 9-11 Truthers nuts: people naturally believe the government version. Such is our political culture: Europeans naturally suspect, Americans naturally believe. Just look how long it took for Americans to believe that Nixon was actually involved in his staff's Watergate shenanigans."

"Fine and well, but what if some State Department flunky slips a photo or two to the AP?" asked the CIA man.

"I take exception to your inference, sir," said the State Intel guy.

The Rainmaker held up pious hands. "In that case, the White House's response is adamant: 'Those are not official photos. We are not responsible, we do not stand behind them. All the official photos have been gathered up, not to be released until 2061.'"

The CIA man shrugged. "All right. So we've got this thing tied off for the short and medium. What was the long?"

"Not much – just a little something now and then to reinforce the basic idea. By then the Truthers will have found cracks in the official story, and it's not a bad idea to head them off at the pass. A year or so on, **the usual movie** will come out. And you have occasional **books or articles or interviews put out by Seals** who claim to have either killed Osama or witnessed it first-hand." He opened his hands as if in offering. "Properly prepared, dear ones, the daring raid on Osama bin Laden in his house in Abbottabad will soon form part of American history."

Silence again, complacent and drowsy now.

The Rainmaker stifled a laugh. *Why don't you all yawn and scratch and take a nice splash in the manure pile?*

"So are we ready to go?" said the White House rep, looking around the table.

"I guess," said the CIA guy grudgingly. "We'll get started on a bin Laden video." He looked at The Rainmaker and raised his laser pointer. **"Right-handed."**

"Thank you," said The Rainmaker. "I think we're done."

People began getting up, stretching their legs and backs. The lady with the pearls opened her purse and looked inside as if to check if anything had been stolen. The White House rep strode over to The Rainmaker and stuck out his hand. "Hey, really: you've *got* to come work for us."

The Rainmaker rose and took the hand. "That's very kind, sir. But I work in narrative – a nice Dickensian pastime in my old age. The Orwellian stuff – 'ignorance is strength,' 'some animals are more equal than others,' all that – I leave to more mature minds."

This photo is from the video made of Osama bin Laden in his Pakistan house and released to the public after the raid.

PIONEER WOMAN

BEHIND HER BACK WE CALLED MRS. GANT "The Neighborhood Manager": unstoppably organizing, brainstorming, prodding. She dragged all us kids into a Neighborhood Olympics one summer and a family volleyball tournament the next. Her worst creation was the "neighborhood prayer" at Thanksgiving, where we all had to join hands in a big circle on her lawn and say one thing that we were thankful for. I can still remember my panic – what to say, how to say it? – as my turn approached, and the panic made my pubescent voice crack. Even worse was her lecture afterwards, her long, broad back bent down to me, that my prayer had been very nice and that those who had laughed were "feelings-challenged." Out of the corner of my eye, I could see my brother gripping his mouth with both hands and dashing around the corner of the house to challenge his feelings in privacy.

Ten years later, still flush with the Holy Grail of human perfectibility, there she was, giving her talk extolling "velvet assertiveness" – role-play exercises to follow. The mother hens in HR adored her and sent round quotes from her talk for weeks.

She hadn't recognized me among the twenty-odd people in the group. During the coffee break, I said hello. This required a shoulder-loosening scoop of courage first; the old instincts die hard.

Her name was no longer Gant, but Purcell; evidently, she was no longer married to the Mr. Gant that I remembered. She had the same angular, athletic figure: thick back and swimmer's shoulders. Her jaw and cheekbones stuck out as gaunt as shins. Her hair was still short and functional, her fingers long and flailing like loose broom bristles.

"Heavenly day, what a small world! Fantastic! Well, and how are *you?*" she exclaimed, for ecstasy had long ago become a way of life for her.

The talk ran its course: college, our families, work. Mrs. Gant – it's impossible even today to think of her as anything else – duly pronounced everything *fantastic,* with the exception of my sister's ovary operation, which rated "horrible." And finally she asked me what I was doing at B and K Distributors. "Didn't you say you majored in Music?"

"With a specialty in composition, to be exact," I said. "Remember I used to take piano lessons from your neighbor?"

"Donna Stevens, yes, fantastic! And you've kept it up! That's *fantastic!*"

"Yeah, well, like most music majors, I ended up taking care of computers. That's what I do here. Get everybody up and running, do a little programming. Keeps the wolves away. I get out by four every day, and I have time for music. I play in a jazz trio, and I write pieces for it."

"Keeps the wolves away? Is that *all?*" Mrs. Gant stared at me, gray eyes blazing. Though her skin had a wide grain, she wore no make-up except for a bit of lipstick, and I had a sudden memory of her two daughters complaining that they were forbidden to even *try* makeup. "How can you *say* that? Hey, you've got to change that attitude. Your work is your life! If your heart is in jazz, *go* for it!"

"Hold on, Mrs. Purcell. It's not so easy to –"

"Judy, please."

"Judy. Look, I need peace of mind when I sit down to the keyboard, and I don't have it if I'm behind on the rent."

"But you can't think about money! That's our problem, you know: we're so materialistic."

"Well, I know plenty of musicians who would give one of their playing fingers for a little romp through materialism."

"But you've got to take your shot!" she cried. "You have a gift, a talent. Why are you wasting it on –"

I tried to head her off, but it was useless. Her voice pounded like a war drum around the long meeting room.

"Don't you think that if you really, really tried, really gave it your all, that you could make it? I mean, imagine it. Close your eyes and think." A sharp nod. "C'mon – close your eyes."

I stifled a sigh and closed them.

"Can't you see yourself, practicing and practicing and practicing? Hour after hour, month after month. And then one day – *don't open your eyes!* – you audition for some really top-flight band that needs a jazz pianist and someone, maybe the manger or maybe just the trumpet player, stands up and shouts, 'That's it! That's just the sound we're looking for! That guy has the hands we want!'"

I wondered if I could open my eyes. I wondered why – how – she still had the power to make grown men close them. Politeness, I figured. Weakness, too. My answer must have been about as wishy-washy, because I don't remember it.

I helped her pick up equipment when she finished, and when we had packed everything into her two big traveling satchels (*Motivate! Inc.*, printed on them), she lowered her rental-car's window, thanked me, and added, "You just think about what I told you. If you ever doubt it, just close your eyes and think of that golden moment when you win that big audition. You can do it, you know. It's in you, I can feel it. Next time I come back here for a presentation, I don't want to see you with the rest of the initiatees," which is what she called those hostage to her four-hour harangue.

And indeed she didn't see me, for I left B and K a year later, having had a torrid affair with the gorgeous comptroller who ended up my wife. But I remembered the encounter, if only because I resented the insinuation that merely earning a living wasn't good enough.

****

And so we jump some ten years into the future. Yours truly with two kids now, the comptroller having turned into a gorgeous freelance accountant, and me head of programming for a small and very sharp women's fashion firm. My band had grown to a quartet with the addition of a jazz guitarist who was explosively – and that's the word, believe me – creative. He composed, I edited his work with input from the bassist and drummer, and a small jazz label recorded our work. We got good reviews in jazz magazines and made enough money to have to declare it on our taxes every year.

Which was why I had flown to Los Angeles to look in on the final cuts of a low-budget (too low) comedy film for which we had made the sound track, mainly an adaptation of our old work. I returned to the airport disgusted: with the exception of the final roll-credits theme, our work had been cut to smithereens. I beefed to the producer, but he sent me packing: "The contract specifically states...."

The lady running flight check-in was Mrs. Gant's daughter Sally. We had time for a quick drink before my flight.

She looked terrific at 37: blond, heeled, controlled – solid class. I saw at first glance why she had run away to California: this way she could wear makeup.

"God, I spent my whole twenties just hiding from her and scraping off layers of guilt. I didn't even tell her what I was doing for three years. And when I finally did?" She made a voice: "'A flight attendant? That's it? Just a *flight attendant*?' Hell, I *loved* it. I've seen every capital in the Orient and most of Europe, what with work and free travel on vacation."

"That's terrific. I envy you."

"Tell Mom. *One time* I spent Christmas with her, and she started giving me the business, and I told her flat out, 'I don't give a good goddamn about being a pilot, CEO of the airline, or anything else.' She flipped. Gave me all that stuff about how if you *really, really try*, you can be anything you want."

"Right. As if all those pro basketball players could be Michael Jordan if they just worked a little harder." I checked the monitor for my flight, and swore – it would board on time. "What's she doing nowadays? Seminar business still going strong?"

"Oh no. God, the opposite. Business dropped way off starting about three years ago. She was bankrupt for a while, and Cindy and I were lending her money. She paid it back eventually. But I think it was all her second ex's money."

"She married a second time, then."

"For a while – to an alcoholic that she helped kick the habit." A sigh and a sip from her wine glass. "Yeah, Mom loses jobs and men. She worked at a half-dozen big corporations – HR stuff. I mean, she must be fabulously convincing in a job interview."

"I'll bet."

"But once she sat down to the desk and computer, she never lasted a year anywhere: personality conflicts, close-minded people who didn't want to listen to her ideas, bosses worried about an ambitious worker coming up the ranks. There was always" – she scratched quotation marks in the air – "a *reason*."

"Not a go-along-to-get-along type, is she?"

"From there, she tumbled down the economic chain: a department store, then a gym, then a convenience store, and now she works in a candy shop."

"*A candy shop?*"

Sally shook her head in wonder. "She's very proud of having raised their sales by 32 percent over the last quarter."

I laughed, checking the monitor again: my flight was boarding. "Does she still give you a hard time about your profession?"

"Never stopped." The voice, plangent and aggravating: "'Motivate your boss! Be assertive, never aggressive. Instruct your boss *assertively* in how to

promote your interests within the company structure.' I tell her, 'Mom, I'm *head of ground operations*
now. A 747 can't push back without *me* giving the
green light.' Forget it. In her eyes, I lack ambition."

****

We jump again, this time fifteen years ahead,
to the end of my report on Mrs. Gant, which I
wouldn't have bothered with at all if it weren't for
this last anecdote.

Over the years, our quartet did a total of five
soundtracks – all for comedy films – each one
more cut to pieces than the last, though the pay
doubled with each one; such is the logic of Hollywood. After the fifth, we said nuts with the whole
thing. The "explosive" guitarist then moved to
L.A., got studio jobs and a big head and an addic-
tion, and out of the blue called me one January
night from a local detox center. Some cousin of
his in Houston had a steady music job for him in
his steak house if he could just get down there.
Could he cadge the one-way airfare? Oh, and he'd
need a ride out to the airport, too.

Well.

The detox was a converted factory building
that had been bought by the city and done over
in late-century institutionalism: walls painted
brown on the bottom half and cream on the upper, a drinking fountain whose burning-cold water
shocked me to the scrotum, busted armchairs like
wounded soldiers strewn about the lounge. It was

winter, and amidst the constant coming-and-goings of residents, workers, ambulances, and delivery men, waves of cold charged through the ground-floor rooms like linebackers blitzing the quarterback.

I was waiting for the guitarist to finish packing up his things and come downstairs when I recognized Mrs. Gant. This was easy because she had never changed her short, sawn-off haircut. She was carrying a tray full of the dirty dishes from someone's breakfast, nearly running with it as if she had a million things to do. I called to her and she braked on a dime, and I introduced myself once again.

"Well! Yes! Heavenly day! And how are *you*? Let me put this in the kitchen real quick."

In a blink, she was back, and steered me through an adjoining doorway into the lounge, where downhearted second-hand paperbacks and an ancient encyclopedia volume slouched across the shelf of a bookcase, otherwise empty. And the cold – God, it was irritating – again and again it plunged through the doorway and smothered you. Mrs. Gant, however, didn't seem to notice, as people who live under flight paths don't notice the roar of airplanes.

"So you're going to pick up poor Calhoun! That's fantastic! He came here absolutely at death's door. I had to be with him twenty-four hours those first two weeks – to be sure he didn't go back to the junk, you know. It was a struggle, but I told him what he needed to hear, and he'll be up and running if he just gets that job in Houston. He can do it. I told him he was a winner. I said he'd be back in Hollywood in a year. That's our contract: in a year, he has to be back working there."

I was going to ask her about the contract but was forced to tell my news: still married, the kids married, grandfatherhood in the offing, a job in a software-consulting firm, two weekend gigs a month for a little extra money and a lot of extra fun, Hollywood over and done with, taxes all paid on the royalties and good riddance.

"But how can you say that after hitting the top!" cried Mrs. Gant. (I still can't call her Judy.)

"Hitting the top and seeing your entire composition chopped down to fifteen bars – those are two very different things," I said.

This staggered Mrs. Gant. She closed her open mouth, stared at the floor on one side of herself – as if looking over the railing of a high bridge. "Well, sounds like it's not all it's cracked up to be," she mused. "Not that it's not all for, you know, for money or anything." She looked up. "But didn't you *fight* for your music? I mean, if you really, really talked to the director or, or the producer or whoever makes the decisions, couldn't you have –"

"Normally the director. No – no chance. That wouldn't –"

"But if you *really* presented your case strongly? Tactfully, of course, but assertively and dynamically, don't you think you could have gotten more of your music into the film? It's all in how you motivate people, you know. The key is..." She went on, gray eyes brilliant in her face only bonier and harder with the years. Here was the haggard pioneer mother crossing the Rockies, months on the trail, determined to reach the legendary green valleys of the Pacific coast, numb to hardship or the cries of hungry children.

I nodded, admitted, shrugged, promised. What else can you do in the face of absolute optimism?

The guitarist saved me by appearing in the lounge doorway. "Hey, man! Thanks so much for –"

"Graduation Day, Calhoun! Congratulations!" Mrs. Gant cried, hugging him. He returned the gesture embarrassedly, one hand clutching the plastic trash liner with all his possessions. He had no guitar, and I wondered if he'd sold his collection of them for heroin.

She pulled away. "And you'll remember your key words, won't you?"

"I'll 'member 'em: SPAN."

"Striving, programming, aspiration, and networking."

Calhoun worked his way past her and shook my hand. "Hey, thanks for comin', man. 'Preciate it."

We walked toward the entrance, Mrs. Gant with her arm around Calhoun's shoulders. "And don't forget your soul, Calhoun," she said. "Because without that, your goals don't have any power behind them. Goal-soul. Remember now. That's your inner force."

"I'll 'member."

He opened the door and Mrs. Gant gave him one last penetrating look. "You can do it, Calhoun. I can feel it. Can't you?"

"Yeah, abs'lutely, Judy. Damn right."

We both said good-bye, though I don't think Mrs. Gant heard me, standing on the front steps like a woman seeing her sailor off to war. "And don't forget the third prong of our strategy, Calhoun," Mrs. Gant called, her breath freezing out as long as her arm. "R.M. and D. You can have all the soul and SPAN you want, but without R.M. and D., it all goes down the drain."

Calhoun waved one last time as he ducked into the car.

I looked at him. "R.M. and D.?"

"Reflection, Meditation and Dreamin'."

"Ah." I started the car and we rolled past Mrs. Gant, still on the front steps, one exiguous hand clutching herself against the minus-10 cold, and waving violently and smiling. "You can do it, Calhoun!" she shouted.

We were silent for a while. The car slid down onto the highway to the airport. The guitarist said, "You know her, man?"

I explained.

"So she had a family, huh? With kids and all?"

"Two daughters."

"Damn! They half-loco too?"

"I ran into one of them some years ago. She wasn't. Can't stand her mom, though."

"Don't surprise me. Damn, that woman talks. Mornin' to night. Runs that place for the city, you know. Last ten years or somethin'. Even lives there – on the top floor? Where she does her therapy too. Pounds your ears till you think you was fuckin' Sup'man."

"I believe it. Hey, what was that she told me about a contract?"

"Oh, *that*." Calhoun pulled a paper out of an inner pocket. "'I, the und'signed, commit myself to returning to my Hollywood music c'reer within a period o' no longer than one year. I also –' Well, there's a bunch o' stuff here I promise not to do, like drink much or smoke and do shit. Then it finishes, 'And I will send a yearly progress report to Judy P. And'son at Christmas to inform her o' my progress.' Signed, Judy and me."

He folded it and tucked it back in a pocket. He stared ahead at the grim highway, the dull blanket of sky. "And then we sign and she pulls out this fuckin' bottle of carb'nated apple juice and shakes 'er up and pops it and gets her rug all wet – we were in her room, you know – and we do a toast and shit...."

His voice broke, and after a moment I heard a loud swallow. I needed an effort not to turn my head. A sob.

"Fuck, man," he whispered hoarsely. "She b'lieves in you more 'n you b'lieve in y'self." He wiped his eyes.

I let a few silent miles go past. "Going to send her the reports?"

"Yeah, sure I'm gonna to send 'em – least for a year or two, I will. Lotta her people do. Says she gets a avalanche o' Christmas cards every year, and it ain't no shit, man. Showed me a big ol' fuckin' box full of 'em. Old ones, goin' back ten years." He gave his eyes a last, definitive wipe. "You can't go and dis'point Judy, man. Yeah, yeah, she's a crazy ol' lady and all, but you just can't."

He said good-bye when we reached the Delta Airlines entrance, said he would pay me back – and he did, with an unnecessary bit of interest, eighteen months later, from L.A. – and ambled shakily away with his trash liner dangling from a hand.

It took me a long time to pull my eyes away from him. "Mrs. Gant," I murmured. "Mrs. Gant. Who would've thought?"

Then cars were honking and an airport cop was fanning my windshield. I hustled away from the drop-off area and out of the airport, planes lancing away on all sides.

\

SHOCCER

THREE OF US – Steve Smith, Fuzzy Millich, and me – tried to watch a soccer game last week. Fuzzy and I were pretty eye-rolly when Steve suggested it. I mean, *soccer*: twenty-odd guys running around a football field dying to use their hands. And the two or three goals that really, actually, finally, in the course of *90 minutes* get made — without the ref calling back the play, without someone falling down and gripping his leg and crying over his wittle boo-boo — those happen when you're at the head pissing out whatever's keeping you awake.

But what the hell. Steve had just got back from this incentive trip to London and had watched a World Cup game between England and France, which he says is a big deal there, like the Lions playing the Vikes on Thanksgiving Day. He said it was a lot better than he'd expected, what with the shouting and fight songs and these quart-sized beers they serve that rock you to your scrotum. (They were watching the game in a "pub," which is like a bar, but cleaner.) Also this really nice guy leaned over from the next table and explained a few of the finer points to Steve and the other sales reps. Max-interesting, he said. Anyways, last Friday it was pretty nice out, so Steve did bratties and kraut on the grill, shooed his kids upstairs, turned on a game between Saudi Arabia and Sweden, and we gave it our best shot.

And I mean that: our best shot. Fuzz and I chucked attitude right overboard – minds open as a new turnpike. Steve pointed out a few things, like how one strategy is to just hail-Mary the ball to the other end of the field and hope for the best, and another is to work it down the sidelines and at the last second boot it into The Area – which is like The Crease in hockey, only bigger – and hope for a header.

Fine and well, interesting as those things go. But hell, in the first half, which is — no joke — forty-five minutes, what happened? Nothing. You read that right: nothing. In the time of almost an entire NFL or NBA game, nothing happened. No goals, no good fights. In the vernacular: nada. Probably the best part was when everybody started arguing with the Japanese (Chinese?) ref, who ended up doing a Nazi salute with a red card, which got everybody even more stirred up, since, as Steve explained, it means a player is out for the duration and nobody's coming in to replace him – a little steep, if you ask me.

"I swear to the ever-lovin' motherfucker himself," Fuzzy burst out as the argument went on and on. "Other countries, man, it's no wonder we gotta go in all the time and sort out their hash. No, no,

I don't care – it's true. Look, what are we seein' here? Half-dozen guys from Saudi Arabia, all with some education, guys who've been around the block a few times – and what do they do? They argue with the ref! What – the guy speaks Saud? He's Chinese, for God's sake. He probably thinks they're telling him, 'Hey, great call.'"

"I guess they do that in Europe, too," said Steve. "The ref always has to be a guy from another country. That way he won't understand anybody."

"Doesn't matter," I said. "Those aren't even Saudi Arabian players, most likely." Sometimes you just gotta be assertive, like my hero Frank Sweldge says. "I'll bet those are Guatemalans. Saudis don't put together a national team: they contract it all out."

"The hell!" cried Fuzzy incredulously.

"On their oil rigs it's all Americans and Kuwaitis and cheap-labor Mexicano-types," I added. "My second cousin down in Florida told me – Jerry. Out on a rig you can't find a Saud for love or money."

"Till it comes time to cash in the crude, of course," Fuzzy sneered.

Then I slipped them a fast one: "Anyways, it's against Islam to kick a leather ball: it could be like their great-grandmother or somebody, reincarnated."

Steve's beer stopped in mid-upswing. "Oh. Jeez." And this when Steve runs a whole territory out of his Piper Cub: Wisconsin to Montana to

Kansas. Try doing that and being home for in time for the kids' hockey games.

Fuzz just stuffed more brattie in his yapper. I didn't blow the whistle on them, since as Frank Sweldge once said, silence is the better part of valor.

But that's not my point here. The point of all this is that the next day, by some incredible co-incidence, we were in Rolf's Drinkery – down on Chestnut? – sipping brew 'cause the temps took a dive and it was doing like minus-50 wind-chill off Lake Superior for a few days, and what shows up on the big screen? Some Brit sports magazine show, and they were talking about that soccer game we'd seen – Saudi Arabia–Sweden? Good thing we'd dropped it, turns out: the final score was 1-0. First, the reporter showed the same one goal from three different camera angles. Fair enough. But then – get this – *they showed what was almost a goal*! I swear this is true. The news report showed a good half-dozen missed shots on goal. *Nothing happening* was a game highlight! We were in like total shock.

"Well, the guy's gotta make up a sixty-second report – producer's counting on it. The hell else is he gonna do?" Steve said lamely. He still felt bad about boring Fuzzy and me with soccer.

"Those people have a problem big-time," said Frank Sweldge. He's a marketing exec for a hockey-equipment company, and he's just like kickass basic 24-7. "That sport can't compete, not in today's market anyways. I've heard there are some decent video-game versions of it — tournaments even — but the park-the-car-and-stand-your-neighbor's-bad-breath version? I wouldn't give it five more seasons to run."

Thao "Tommy" Chhung said, "My dad loves soccer. He watches a game just about every day after lunch." But you gotta give Tommy a little slack here, seeing as how his father had been a Laotian Army colonel around the fall of Saigon. He'd led his village all the way to Thailand, and only half of the 1200 people made it out alive, so he likes things quiet. A sport where nothing happens is probably right up his alley.

Gib Henderson spoke up: "Know what they oughta do there, see, is widen the goals a few feet."

"A few yards, more like – shit!" said Fuzzy, and Steve swamped his face in the suds real fast.

And that's how the whole thing got started. We're all pulling down brew and all of a sudden the ideas just start jumping out like welder's sparks. Till Don "Shally" Shalishasvilli said, "Hey! Why don't we write this stuff down and reach it out to the NSL or whatever they have?"

"With all due respect, Shally: their country, their deal. Leave 'em be," said Ferd Gaarslund, who's always trying to be "an influence," which he figures he's entitled to because he has a subscription to *The New Yorker*. He can kiss my netherworlds.

"Tell the Japanese and the Germans, Ferd," said Frank Sweldge. "International stuff, that's like my old Harley: great when it works." Another piledriver that I personally thought was like max-fucking awesome. I guess that's the kind of wisdom you pick up outguessing the markets all day.

OK, without further to-do, here's our list:

1) *Put two balls on the field.* This was Frank's idea, and it just kicks ass. We calculated that every game would average between twenty and thirty goals, and you know what that means: Showtime! Also, the goalkeeper would have to be blocking shots all game long, which would really boost his productivity.

2) *Give the players some type of helmet and body protection.* Chalk this one up to Rolf. Not only would this allow players to block and hit, like in football, but, much more important, it would keep players from getting hurt and falling down and gripping their knees like the only option was amputation. That happened twice in the half-game we saw, and it was just max pathetic, especially because after rolling around on their backs for five minutes the guys just got back up again and kept playing. Besides, it gives a totally downside image of their countries, and God knows we have enough of those.

3) *Make a rule that at least three women from each team have to be on the field at any one time.* Tim "Z" Zark had this idea at the same time as Bill Castellini, and they had to compromise on the number; so both of them have to get credit. Frank added that you could branch that into all kinds of merchan-

dising, like team thongs and bras, training-camp reality shows and photo ops for the team webpage. (Talk about vision – wow.)

4) Put a small pond in the middle of the field. Who else but Frank? His idea was to put a pond 30 feet square at the center of the field. Not deep — like the water jump in steeplechase running. Kevin Podzuweit pointed out that it would be hard to kick a ball in a pond, but Frank, with a marketing exec's patience, just looked up to His Maker and asked for help: "That's the point, Kevvers," he sighed. "Splashing? Women? Hello!" Maybe only the women would be allowed in to duke it out for the ball, he said, but you'd want to really focus-group that one for family issues first. Whatever. Point is, put six women and a pond on the field, and the U.S. soccer market is going to grow like mosquitoes in a junkyard tire. Who knows? With the right seed money, you might even end up with a North Atlantic Soccer Organization. Talk about win-win! International stuff is great when it works, just like the master said.

Well, those are the ideas of twelve good men at Rolf's Drinkery in North Hoot, Minnesota. We want to emphasize that we totally respect others' culture and that only they can manage this issue as they think best. We don't want to see their sport disappear any more than they do. In fact, if they don't even want to call this "soccer" anymore, we fully understand and would like to suggest this name: "shoccer," a combination of "showtime" and "soccer." (Frank again – Jesus!) All of us at Rolf's pledge to give the new sport a full-frontal open-minder, bratties and the works, once the changes come on line. Seriously.

Now if somebody can get me the address of the NSL or whatever they have, I'll reach this right out.

ALAN THE NEWSBOY

SONNY FRENCH WAS TALKING to his protector in the narco division, and things were not going well.

"French, you got some imagination: us breakin' in through your *basement*?" the narcotics detective chuckled. "Okay, first off, lemme put your mind at ease: any arrest resulting from a police plot to break into your house would be totally illegal. Second, no police force works that way unless maybe you're the whole-nine-yards Pablo Escobar. By which I mean, what are you? A small-timer that peddles to the movers and shakers. Everybody knows who you are, but any time someone around the office talks about taking you down, I just remind them that you're not a pusher standing on the edge of a playground, you don't go door-to-door selling to underaged hookers. If one of *your* clients sniffs his brains to hell, nobody cares. Let's work on takin' down who *needs* takin' down. So relax."

"I'd relax if my fuckin' basement wasn't knee-deep in water with more comin' in every minute."

"Yeah, how the hell did it break? Your place is in one of those new housing developments. The walls must be solid concrete down there."

"Insurance guy said cinder brick reinforced with vertical steel rods every three feet."

"Water seepage that built up and finally broke through — that'd be my guess."

"Yeah, except there was no water stain on the wall around the hole, I never smelled any mould or damp down there, and it's hardly rained a fuckin' drop all summer. Plus, when did it happen? While we were out of town for two weeks."

"'We,' huh? You still with that babe with the Silly Putty chest?"

Sonny clicked the phone off but kept up a steady patter, walking up and down the hallway outside the bedroom in case Nicole was listening. "I'll tell you what to check and when to check it, asshole. I can always cut you the fuck off and buy myself another...." But at that moment Nicole turned on the hair blower. With a huff, he slapped the cell phone shut. He expected more grovelling from a man he paid.

"How come everybody thinks I was born to get shitted on?" he groused.

He wandered out to the bedroom terrace. The mid-August sun was falling, and the shadow from the woods beyond his high backyard wall was slipping towards him over the long sheet of grass with its two slouched, braced-up saplings and, here and there like electronic mushrooms, the movement and infra-red sensors, each with a green and a red light that irritatingly reminded him of Christmas. He'd only bought the place, boring and suburban, to look responsible to his family. He smoothed back his hair and re-tied his signature leather cord with the skulls on the ends.

"Problems are for the poor, for fuck's sake," he murmured. "Everything's fine."

He gave the cord a final jerk and did a few push-ups against the railing, thinking of how he smart he had been to buy a house at the end of a cul-de-sac — no one in sight. He loved to have his girls out here, bend them naked over the fat, round railing and take them from behind — give it to them hard — while they hung in space, boobs hanging and flopping. Some liked it and others were told to like it. Nicole, his current girl, whom he had been with for a record-breaking seven months, liked everything — too much.

Nicole: red-haired, short and broad. "Yup, I'm all hips and tits, honey," which she framed in Spandex when she wasn't walking around the house topless. She came after him continually, three times a day, jerking off his pants and scissoring him with her legs or simply engulfing him. Constantly exhausted sexually, it took Sonny Herculean concentration to reach orgasm; sometimes he couldn't, and that displeased her. In Nicole's eyes, real men were infinitely virile.

She spent his money — some earned, most inherited — on clothes, restaurants, shows, jewelry (none fake), and her new Porsche 911; but had also brought homey warmth to the place, putting up curtains, buying paintings at galleries, throwing out the art-deco junk and getting an elegant sofa set for the living room.

And when the bill came: "So whaddaya want? Mr. Sonny French just drank dry martinis with a Grammy nomination and the Yankees top batter" — she came up and put her arms around him, throwing back her long hair and looking up from his chest — "he's got the NYPD wrapped 'round his little finger, he's got the best pair o' tits in New York to squeeze, and he's gonna live like some Macon pig farmer?" She shoved him onto the sofa, still covered in plastic from the shop, and went to work on him. "Now am I right or am I right?" she inquired from his thighs.

She was, she was. And she could cook anything and organize a party and make other men burn to be in his shoes. She was only twenty-one — eight years younger than Sonny — and she was perfect.

He feared constantly that she would leave him. She'd shacked up with an NBA player for six months and walked out on him "when he got cut and hadda take a contrack playin' with some horseshit outfit in France. I said he can take a loser girl with him, and there's lots of 'em, with nice print blouses and tits like golf balls. Find 'em at any hairdresser's."

The comment troubled Sonny like a cold sore on the lip that one cannot stop licking. If he broke the image of the exquisitely cool night-club back-slapper, she might well take that new Porsche, which he had grandly registered in her name, and speed away right out of his life. Only once, he had told her he was just too tired for sex — after two sessions already that afternoon — and had felt her deciding for the entire next day if she should stay or not. He threw a twenty-thousand-dollar ruby-studded watch into the breach and survived; but he never refused her advances again.

Leaning out, he looked down at the strip of gravel that separated the grass from the house's foundation. There, at the midpoint of the house, he could see a hammock-like depression in it, three steps long out into the grass, right where the basement hole was. Was the insurance agent right? "Any reason someone would want to get into your house, Mr. French?" he'd asked, looking at the hole from the basement stairway. "I mean, I wouldn't put money on it — and we'll cover everything, don't you worry about a thing — but, you know, movement sensors aren't everything, and I wouldn't be a bit surprised if someone'd found a way to slip past your yard security and then — whatever — cut through the sod, dig down and break in. Most likely it was just the builder's bad: freak water breakage. But then why isn't there a humidity stain around that hole? And see there on the top rim of it? Perfectly dry. Sure nothing's gone?"

Sonny was sure. As soon as he had discovered the problem, he had waded into the "guest room" with its massive water bed to check things over. At a glance he could see that his three long shelves of porn — many of them his home-made titles — were intact. He opened the full-length mirror and found the camera behind it high and dry in its place. The ground and upper floors of the house, from the basement door on, were covered by a security system worthy of Cartier's.

"Would you just put it the fuck outta your mind?" Sonny whined quietly to the backyard. "Tomorrow they'll come and pump the place out, replace the furnace and A/C. In a week, it's history."

History: time loping along over an endless plain. He did more pushups, stood up, sighed. What the hell did people *do*? Except when he was shopping or in a club or making love, he was always bored. All day he waited for night to come, when he could dress up, roar into New York in the Ferrari, check out the action and sell some powder. But actually *do* — what the hell was that? He picked up the day's newspaper, which Nicole had left on the deck chair, and looked blankly at the headlines: *Dem Convention to Crown Obama Candidate. First Black Candidate in U.S. History.* Sonny huffed and tossed it back on the chair. "Who gives a shit?" he muttered.

Nicole sauntered out to the terrace wearing only panties, fluffing her waist-length curls, a waterfall of red and purple.

Not again. Shit! thought Sonny.

"You finish with the insurance guy?" she said.

"Yeah. Said the break was probably from water built up against the wall. Genius, huh? Wouldn't get his pants wet: just looked at the hole from the stairs."

Nicole leaned over the terrace and pointed down at the depression, her bulbous breasts swinging out. "Zat from the hole?"

"Yeah." He watched her breasts, his groin stirring, though its dull ache informed him that he was probably incapable after the three sessions yesterday and the one that morning before they caught their flight.

"Betcha got a killer aquifer down there. I got an uncle had one under his tractor shed. Unbalanced the slab and bust it in two." She pointed out past the lawn. "And that crick out there behind your wall is feedin' it."

"I'm gonna sue the builder till he screams if he sold me a bad house," Sonny groused for her.

"Damn right. Let people piss on you, and you may as well open a toilet shop. My daddy always used to say that." She stretched her arms, her breasts jutting forward; Sonny braced for the inevitable. "Damn, I hate a cold shower, and no air-conditionin' in this heat. When they gonna come to fix ev'thing, baby? This ain't no way to live: comin' home and findin' the place a shithouse."

"Tomorrow — insurance guy's gonna fix it up."

"Well, we're gonna hafta go into town and find ourselves a hotel. How 'bout if we go to the Ritz? It's nice. Ever been there? Great place for messin' up the sheets," she added with a grin.

Her hand dropped down to the elastic waist-band of his athletic pants, and he threw himself on her and kissed her savagely, grasping for an excuse: food — that was it. He was hungry, they should call out for food. That would buy him some time at least.

He was saved by the bell — or at least the dong-ding-dong-ding alarm that signaled a "friend-ly entry": some authorized person was coming through the front gate. Which was strange, since the cleaning lady had the month off and no gro-ceries had been ordered. "How 'bout checking that out, baby?" Sonny said. "I'm sick o' that damn door and everyone who comes through it."

"Okay, honey," she said simply, releasing his member and letting the pants back up. "But y'owe me one."

"You owe me a million, baby," he said, and her skeptical smile made him shudder.

Zipping on a track suit, Nicole went down-stairs to the front hall. The security monitor, which blinked NEWSBOY at the bottom, showed the de-livery boy coming up the walk; he had an entry-code number because he delivered the morning paper. But now he had nothing in his hands except the little book he used for collecting the monthly bill. The canvas bag for keeping his money swung from the belt loop of his cut-off blue jeans.

All of which astonished Nicole: Sonny had convinced him never to collect for the paper and to pay for Sonny's subscription himself. Nicole had been there ten weeks earlier when the convincing was done.

****

Sonny, in a vile, coked-up mood, in the middle of a hammering screw on the living-room carpet. The gate alarm sounds and in a moment, the house doorbell rings. Sonny runs to the hall and looks at the monitor and swears. "It's the Boy Scout with his fucking little receipts here to collect!"

"Let it go, baby," Nicole whisper-calls from the rug. "Light's on but nobody's home."

Sonny whirls and shakes back his hair, grinning. "No. No, we're gonna fix this little shit. C'mere — fast." She snatches a bathrobe off the sofa. "This is gonna be fuckin' great!" Sonny chuckles.

"What is?"

"Get him downstairs to the guest room and shake your tits at him. Heat him up and then do him." He grabs a pair of jeans off the floor and pulls them on. "But stall him. Give me a minute to get the lights and sound set up."

Nicole stares. "Screw the — ? He ain't even old enough to — "

"Fuck that. He's fifteen — he told me. Whaddaya think fifteen-year-olds think of night and day? He'll love it." He dashes for the basement door.

She laughs. "You are one nasty s.o.b., baby!"

Getting him downstairs with a can-you-help-me-lift-something story, she slips off her bathrobe. The kid — was it Alex? Albert? — can't believe it. Nicole poses curvy-sweet as the kid's eyes bug out like beachballs.

Tits that'll stop a train, she thinks.

"Hey!" the kid exclaims with alarm — and reaches for the bathrobe on the bed.

"It's all right, baby," she purrs, pulling his trembling hands to her breasts. "It's all for you. Sonny's a thousand miles away, and I need a little lovin'. You *do* know how to do it, don't you?"

He is a tall, fair boy: a heavy sweep of bangs to one side, deep-set blue eyes and a bright pink lower lip. His pale cheeks are downy with three sweet pimples on his chin. Nicole touches his smooth neck and fingers the sexy lower lip. *Yeah, I can get into this just fine. Gonna be steam comin' outta this boy's ears by the time I'm through with him.*

"Yeah, sure. I know," the boy croaks bravely. "I know — " he swallows — "all about that. But, y'know, I don't know you, y'know...."

"What?" she giggles.

"I mean, like, you're Mr. French's girlfriend and all. And besides, I sort of have this girlfriend, y'know. Or at least" — another swallow — "we, like, go out sometimes."

"Bet yer girlfriend doesn't have *these*, does she?" Nicole pulls his limp arms up to her again. The kid's hands lock automatically over her thick breasts.

"No, she sure doesn't," he says with a tripping giggle. "But you know, it wouldn't be, y'know, right and all." Another gulp. "And safe sex and all that." He takes his hands away, though slowly.

"You sure?" Nicole says, posing and rumpling her red hair over her head. *Just feast your eyes, buddy-boy.* "Bodies like this don't come along every day, baby."

He is trying to look away but can't, and Nicole loves it. His voice is barely a whisper, punctuated with gulps. "I mean like, it's not that you're not nice and all, but it, y'know, just wouldn't be.... Um, was there something you wanted me to lift?"

Nicole reaches for his hands again and they come. "Just these. They're so heavy, you know. I need someone to take the weight offa me a while. They're pretty nice, doncha think?"

"Yeah." Another giggle.

She steps forward and pulls his head down and kisses the mouth that tastes of licorice, and clamps her teeth on that juicy lower lip. Little by little she gets his T-shirt and shorts off, and suddenly he is all elbows and hot mouth. They spill onto the bed and he roars into her.

"Was that okay for you?" he blurts a minute later. He wipes his forehead, his blond bangs dark with sweat. "I mean, it was really kind of my first time and all, and it was just kind of hard to hold it once I, y'know, got going." He puffs out. "God, that was great!"

Then Sonny bursts out of the closet behind the mirror, laughing. And now so does she.

The boy springs off the bed, looking around in panic.

"Surprise!" shouts Sonny, swinging away the mirror on its hinges. "You're on Candid Porn Camera!"

"Hey, what kinda deal is this?" he squawks, eyes going wet.

"Just a little joke, baby," says Nicole, giggling. "Don't take it serious."

"*Don't take it serious?* You just filmed me with — "

"Shut up and listen, kid. From now on, you're paying for my *Daily Journal*. Unless you want me to put this film on the Net for everyone to see: Alan seduced live!"

The kid is snatching up his shoes, the skinny arms heaving things up to his chest — awkward, since he is trying to keep his groin covered. He clutches the little money bag in one hand and the collection book in the other. "This isn't fair! I never did anything to you! Or you," he adds to Nicole.

"Well, that's what you get for coming around collecting on me all the time!"

"C'mon! I have to, for Pete's sake!" The kid runs out, his sweet buttocks wobbling. "The paper makes me!"

"I don't want to see you around here anymore with your fucking little collection bag," calls Sonny. "Get it? From now on, my paper's free. And don't you dare stop delivering. Unless you want to be the youngest porn star on the Net."

"Okay, all right!" comes the teary voice from the stairway.

And now the boy was coming across the front yard consulting his little book. He planned to collect.

****

Alan the newsboy crossed the yard, his blond bangs flapping above his right temple. He'd changed. He looked bigger. But of course, nearly three months had passed, and a fifteen-year-old would be. But his arms and shoulders, especially: farmboy muscles, Nicole noted, that started at the base of the neck and made a single, chiseled line down to the elbow. He was thumbing through his little black collection book, and the little white-canvas money sack swung with legal frequency at his side. She opened the front door and the first thing she looked for was that beautiful lower lip — and was disappointed. It was dull and chapped; it reminded her of the corn-tasslers back home who finished their day covered with dust.

"Well! Didn't expect to see *you* again!" she said with a smile.

"Yeah, I guess." He looked at her a long moment: the deep-set blue eyes could not quite hate her.

Boy's nuts about you, Nicole thought. *You were his first time, and the little shit hasn't stopped thinking about your 44s all summer.* And then, shocking her: *What a slut you are, Niki. A total, two-fisted slut* — the thought squirreled into her mind like a ray from a car headlight.

He looked over her into the house. "I have to collect for the *Daily Journal*. Is Mr. French in?"

"Thought *you* were payin' for it," Nicole taunted. "Last I heard, you were runnin' up the steps, sayin'" — she made a burbling, crying noise — "'All right, all right, I'll pay for it m'self!'"

His face, his whole body, were rigid. "Well, I'm not doing — I'm not going to do that now," he said. He consulted the collection book. "Mr. French owes me for May, June, July and today's paper."

"Well, I guess Sonny's gonna put our little screw on the Net." She grinned. "You know, if I was you, I'd ask fer a percentage. I know *I'm* gonna. People pay good money fer that, y'know."

The boy shrugged his heavy boxer's shoulders. "If he wants — " a swallow — "he can do what he wants."

Nicole laughed, her massive hair shaking. "Oh, *there's* the quote of the day!" She turned around and shouted, "Baby, come on down here! That newspaper kid's here ta collect and he says that if you want, you can do what you want!"

"*What the fuck?*"

Sonny jogged down the steps and came to the door. "Well, look at this! Our local porn star. Come back for a second take?"

"I just want to collect for the paper," the boy said glumly. He raised the collection book like a prayer book, held open between the thumbs. "It's

167 dollars. That's for three months. Today's paper is the only one for August."

Sonny nodded. "A hundred sixty-seven bucks. Adds up, huh?" he said to Nicole.

"Sure does, baby." She shook her head. "Looks like some people just don't care nothin' for common decency. Just let 'er all hang out on a web page."

The boy watched, inert as a shell, big shoulders hunched behind his head.

"But I thought we had a deal, Alex. Remember our deal?"

"*Alan*. I didn't make any deal."

"No? Then how come you haven't come to collect the bill?" Sonny challenged him.

"Well, because, because you weren't here when I came and...and that's that."

"'And...and that's that,'" Sonny imitated, laughing.

Alan's voice rose slightly. "If you don't pay me, I go to the newspaper and they're gonna send a guy from the collection agency, and then they take you to court, and those people don't mess around." he blurted in a set speech. "Now: it's 167 dollars. If you don't want to pay, I'll just call the branch manager and he can take it from — "

"Hey-hey, calm down here, Casanova. Nobody said they weren't going to pay you. We're going to pay him, aren't we, Niki?"

Nicole grinned. "Damn right, baby. We're gonna pay this boy in full." She unzipped the jacket of her track suit and pulled it open. "How 'bout we just do it again, and that'll put ever'thing ta rights?"

Alan's face bloomed red.

"Go ahead, Alan," Sonny snickered, turning sideways. "I won't watch this time — promise."

He and Nicole chuckled.

Alan stepped away. "All right. I'll call the branch manager."

Sonny grabbed his arm; for it occurred to him that to be in the crosshairs of a collection agent might be bad for business. "Hold on, hold on. We'll pay. Fuck, Alan, it's not like you have to go and call the cops on us. We're law-abiding citizens."

"Alan-baby, you're just no fun anymore!" said Nicole, zipping the jacket up again.

Alan rolled his eyes in irritation. "Sue me."

"Niki, go get some money. If Alan here wants to be a porn star, that's his good right." It was an expression of his father's. "How much did you say it was?"

"A hundred sixty-seven dollars."

Sonny turned to Nicole. "Get 'im a couple o' centuries, wouldja, baby? Condoms aren't getting any cheaper." He jerked his thumb at Alan. "He's one of these safe-sex guys, you know."

"Didn't seem to stop him last time 'round," Nicole giggled over her shoulder.

Sonny stepped close and said in a man-to-man voice, "You talked this over with your parents, Alan? That's what I like to see: the whole family pulling together like a unit."

"Um, yeah. They said it's okay."

"Great." Sonny poked him lightly on the arm and whispered, "And, Alan, if you're thinking I'm some bleeding-heart motherfucker who *really wouldn't do a thing like that....*" He stepped away. "You're trippin'. 'Cause I will."

The fingers moved on the black plastic of the collection book, leaving wet finger marks. A shrug. Then, with effort, Alan found his voice: "Did she make copies, like, to send out to her friends?"

"Hey — there's an idea: we'll make copies, you know, as demos," laughed Sonny, leaning on the doorframe. "Send 'em out to porno-vid producers. Big money in that."

Alan looked down at his book. "Yeah."

"Hey, and another idea!" Sonny swatted him on the shoulder. "Go talk with your *counselor* if you need to! Do they still have those — high-school counselors?"

"Well, yeah. Except that school doesn't start till next week."

"Oh yeah — no school. Well, it doesn't matter. I can always hold the film till then. Probably have to look up your school's web page and send some frames over there directly — get the ball rolling a little. They have a web page, don't they?"

"Yeah, they have one." He looked up with frank challenge in his eyes. "Go ahead."

Then Sonny got it. *That* was the strategy: Alan was a minor. They prepare the legal ground, let the film come out, then hit Sonny full blast with civil and criminal suits. And try to run Nicole up on some kind of sex-with-a-minor charge.

Well, fuck if I'm gonna walk into that one, Sonny thought, shaking his head sadly. "Have it your way, Alan: I'll just have to send that video out to a little place in Concord I know that specializes in turning porno tape into digital. They'll cook it any way I tell them. I'll have 'em blur out Nicole's face, change her voice, and nobody'll be the wiser."

Alan wiped his sweaty forehead.

"Sure you still wanna collect on me?"

"Yeah."

They heard Nicole coming. Alan's hands flew into action. He tore, along the perpendicular dotted lines, the little green ticket-receipts in his collection book, and handed them to Sonny. Nicole put two hundred-dollar bills in Alan's hand.

"Little tip for that nice piece o' ass you gave me, baby," said Nicole with a wet grin.

Alan looked at the two bills, splayed in one hand, and for a moment, Sonny thought he was going to give them back. Then he folded the bills the way the poor do — in half, then in half again, which made Sonny suck in his gut with pleasure — and slid them into his canvas collection bag. "Thank you. Have a good day," Alan said, stepping backwards, bangs flapping as he jerked the strings of his collection bag tight.

"They'll understand," Sonny continued. "Family's are great about that. I'm not so sure about friends, though. Friends can be pretty rough. Especially high-school age. But hell, you just tell 'em there are all kinds of great new career ops, and porn is just one more of 'em."

"Okay." Alan turned around toward the gate, then back, turned forward, turned back. Sonny and Nicole started to laugh. Finally, he set his feet and spoke:

"So is engineering. I'm gonna be an engineer, y'know."

Then he was away, sprinting over the grass instead of following the swerving walk, which set off the security alarms. He punched his number into the console at the gate and jerked it open. Whirling, he pointed a thick, mannish finger at them. "And I'm cutting off your subscription, Mr. French! From now on, you want the *DJ*, you can just drive up to the gas station for it!" As the door hummed shut, he shoved away on his bicycle.

"*Engineer?*" Nicole said to Sonny's stiff face.

****

She left him not ten minutes later, jewelry stuffed into the suitcase she hadn't unpacked from their trip to California. "Musta spent the whole summer walkin' across that grass and figurin' out how to get around them alarms!" she yelled down the stairway to the basement. "And you sittin' there like a dumbshit with a timebomb like that."

Sonny, standing in the water, was shuffling through the hundreds of video tapes on the shelves. *Newsboy.* He was sure he had labeled it

Newsboy. But sometimes he was too tired to put tapes back in alphabetical order....

"*Paperboy?*" he muttered, and moved down to the P section.

Her voice hammered down the steps: "How long's it gonna be before the paddywagon and a lawyer wavin' a lawsuit at us come screechin' up to this place? Huh, baby? Ten minutes? An hour? Soon as the cops finish their coffee and get in the squad car, that's for sure."

"Keep you pants on," said Sonny. "They woulda come already."

"Maybe they woulda, maybe not. Maybe Alan just wanted to see the stupid look on our faces before he calls 'em. Whatever. Thing is, this is all hip deep in shit and sinkin' fast." Her keys jingled as she snatched them out of the security box.

"You're sinkin' a lot faster than me, baby. It's *your* face and tits on that tape, not mine."

"And who was filmin', smartass? The man in the moon? Me and li'l Alan are going make sure your butt gets fried right along with mine."

"Your word against mine," Sonny shouted back, though she just laughed her head off.

"Oh, that's a good one: 'Your word against mine.' I'm gonna have to tell the folks at the club about that one."

"I see you hangin' around the clubs and I'll cut your fuckin' tits off! And without 'em you're just one more — "

"Oh, you'll never see these tits again, baby. I'm just gonna swing by to say adios. Think I'll head down to Miami. Coupla days, I'll have a new man between my knees screamin' for more. Maybe I could get that Alan to come. Now *there's* a boy with guts — not to mention plenty o' juice in those smooth li'l balls o' his. Gal gets tired o' dry fucks, y'know."

"Come here and say that, bitch!" he screamed, charging through the water to the basement steps, but the water slowed him down, and by the time he had run up the steps and outside, she was revving the Porsche as the driveway gates opened. It squealed away.

And this made him think: the security computer. It recorded everyone's entries and exits at the front gate. When had the little fucker done it?

"I'll find the break-in tape and hang a counter-lawsuit on him that he won't pay off for fifty fucking years!" Sonny snarled.

He went to the security closet beside the front door, leaving a tattered trail of muddy footprints behind — but that was the maid's problem — and opened the computer. A few taps on the keyboard and mouse brought him to all movements of July and the first two weeks of August. The number that Alan punched on the front-gate lock was recorded twice every morning at around five-thirty a.m., until two weeks earlier when he and Nicole went to California. Then just one more entry that morning. The intervals, however, never varied:

the entries and exits, listed in separate columns on the screen, were roughly forty seconds apart. He clicked on the video for that morning's entry, but it showed nothing remarkable: Alan slipped through the front gate and, following the walkway, approached the front door. He stuffed the folded newspaper through the door slot, turned around and left: 37 seconds.

Sonny stroked back his hair and re-tied it, thinking. A bird squawked outside, startling him. Christ, he hated being alone. "This is fucking impossible: he couldn't get ten feet before the infra-reds and movements sensors would've picked him up....."

He turned off the alarm system and walked around to the backyard and examined the depression near the house. He tugged at the sod in a wide radius. No, nothing had been dug up. He shuffled the gravel there along the edge of the house, getting all the way down to the plastic sheeting beneath it: all intact.

For fifteen minutes in the August dusk, darkened by the coastline of an approaching cloudbank, Sonny walked aimlessly around the long bare backyard, head down, studying the ground. Beyond the back wall, the evening songs of the woods — itself re-zoned for a new housing development — began at fits and starts, like an orchestra tuning up; the humidity gripped him in a bear hug. Finally, he stopped, hands stuffed in his back pockets, head swinging slowly from side to side.

"How in the living *fuck*...?"

He peered at the depression, and then to where it vaguely pointed, at the back wall. "No. No, that'd be impossible. That must be thirty fuckin' yards."

Then he had an old pair of tennis shoes on his feet and was carrying an aluminum ladder that he'd never used, jabbing it against the concrete back wall like a pole vaulter.

At first, from atop the wall, all he saw were the steep earthen banks and the creek sliding briskly along a ten-foot-wide trough, small fish squirming here and there, low gruff shrubs, pines hanging over the other bank, their roots sticking out like knobby knees. Nothing else. He would have climbed back down right there, except for — of all things — a small kiddy mirror set into a stretch of pewter-colored clay on the opposite bank, a hopeful dot that, from his high angle, reflected the bright creek water.

"Aw, what the hell," he muttered, and pulled the ladder over the wall, climbed down, and in scuffing little jumps, descended the ten-foot bank to the flat area along the creek.

"Well, that was a useless bit of — "

His eye fell on black plastic tubing snaking along the ground and followed it to a tingling light, just downstream. Twirling away a foot under the surface, it was a water pump: a bicycle wheel rim set horizontally on an iron rod pounded into the creek bed. A dozen plastic beach shovels wired into the spokes caught the current of water. On its top side, also under water, the bike rim was attached to an an articulated arm, and this to a pumping mechanism: a plastic toy accordion set in a jury-rigged wooden frame with four stout little legs. One end of the accordion was impaled on the cheap corrugated-plastic electrical housing he'd seen.

He noticed four deep round depressions in the bank there. He lifted the pump out and set its four little legs in the depressions; they fit perfectly. Still pumping, the accordion gaspingly emptied itself of water and began pumping air.

I'm gonna be an engineer.

"Fuck me," Sonny said in wonder. "Fuck. Me."

The tubing led to a tarp laid over the steep bank. He kicked it away and stared: a tunnel running under his fence, two feet wide and almost as high. The tubing disappeared into it. Until a moment ago, it was pumping water into his basement.

"Motherfucker," he murmured, though it was an epithet of amazement as much as accusation.

Just inside the tunnel, he saw a surgical mask and bits of supermarket cardboard; a little train of six yellow beach pails sat nailed atop two wooden slats, these curved up on both ends like sled runners. They slid into the tunnel on two tracks embedded with flat stones and pebbles. By them lay a roller-skater's hard knee pad, its strap broken. And a finger-long tube that, after he turned it over a few times, proved to be a laser pointer.

"What the ....?" Sonny repeated. "What in the ....?"

He lay down flat and looked into the tunnel, flashed the laser into its darkness to no effect. Sawn-off branches held up roof supports of cheap plywood and doubled cardboard at three-foot intervals. He wriggled in as far as his chest and quickly backed out. "Like *fuck* I'm going in there."

And as he sat up, he saw the little mirror on the opposite bank. It had a plastic pink backing — the kind of thing a five-year-old would use. On a hunch, he pointed the laser: the beam shot back at his midriff. Of course: it was a beacon to keep the tunnel straight and level.

"But what the fuck difference does it make?" he griped, standing up and looking around. "You tunnel your way in, bust the foundation with whatever, get in, grab the vid, crawl back out. So fucking what? I could have made a hundred copies already of the — "

Then he remembered Alan's elliptical question about copies of the tape and his own stupid answer.

"Motherfucker! I'm going to kick his — "

Then he saw his name — Alan the newsboy's name. It had come and gone so quickly as he raged around that he needed to look again. There it was: down the creek and jammed in some rocks. Sonny walked right into the water, which rose as far as his thighs, and waded some twenty feet down the creek. With a wrench, he jerked a board out from where it had drifted. It was a piece of thin plywood, as long as his arm and perhaps a foot wide.

Enormously, in fat, black marker, was written Alan Stahlbacher. Under this, a long wavering arrow pointed to his left. A thick string to hang the sign from was tied to holes at each end of the board.

"The little shithead wrote his *name* on it!" Sonny laughed. "I'll have your ass! By the time my lawyers get through with you, your mother will be offering to suck my...."

But this was all wrong. Why the sign? Why incriminate himself? And why the arrow? He made his way back to the tunnel, and saw that to the right side of it a bush grew out of the bank; two small branches had been stripped of leaves. Bending down, Sonny hung the sign on them; the arrow now pointed right at the tunnel.

"Jesus fuckin' Christ," Sonny blurted, staggering backwards. "For Chrissakes, not *that*."

It had hung there all summer, just in case on some humid July afternoon the earth had collapsed on Alan ten feet under the lawn, so that eventually someone might find him and his body be recovered: evidently, he had dug his forty-yard tunnel all alone and never said a word to anyone, not a brother, a sister, nor even his best friend.

Sonny stared at the sign for a long time, as if it were a gravestone. "For fuck's sake, it was just a, a *vid*, that's all. It's not like...." He stepped backwards, stumbled and sat down on the bank.

Which is where he stayed until nightfall, his feet in the stream, hands absently frittering the plywood sign and tossing the pieces one by one into the creek. "It was just a vid, that's all," he muttered every minute or two.

And to his irritation he repeated this phrase for months whenever he was alone: driving into New York, peeing, tying his shoes, foraging for something interesting on the Internet. His head would jerk up of its own accord and the phrase would bubble out his mouth: "Fuck's sake, it was just a dumb little vid." He seemed to be cursed with the phrase. Like a bad tooth or a smell, it would not leave him alone.

Not, that is, until a sleepless 5 a.m. in April when, having said it twice that night, he lurched out of bed and stood at the upstairs hallway window in his bathrobe and slippers. He stood staring down the long still street milky and dream-like under the streetlamps.

And after a half-hour, he saw a movement. Yes, it was Alan the newsboy, trotting in diagonals across the street as if lacing its shoes. Now he went back to his bike, swept up the kickstand, and continued forward to the next group of houses.

Sonny went to his safe and began throwing rubber-banded rolls of money into a pillowcase. When it had a satisfying weight, he went downstairs and out through the garage.

"Hi, Alan."

Getting off his bike, the boy flinched, looked around, saw him coming down the driveway, its gate rumbling aside. "Hi," he said flatly. He swatted down the kickstand with this foot and jerked a newspaper out of his saddle bags. He folded it in thirds and shoved it through the neighbor's mail slot in the wall.

Sonny walked up and handed over the pillow-case. "Here — keep it." He took a step back, then added, looking up the street, "I thought it was just a dumb little vid, see. I didn't figure you'd...you know. You got rid of it, didn't you?"

Alan was holding out the pillowcase, wary, as if it had something live in it. "Yeah."

Sonny nodded and walked away.

"Wow! Hey, thanks, Mr. French. *Holy moley!* That's...there's...."

Sonny flapped a hand without turning around and trudged up his driveway, head down like a hunter looking for tracks.

"I'll restart your subscription, okay?"

"Don't bother," Sonny answered over his shoulder. "I'm movin' out soon as I sell this dump."

"Oh. Where you movin' to?"

Sonny entered the garage and hit the button, and the driveway gate and garage door closed be-hind him. "Somewhere different," he murmured. "Somewhere so totally fuckin' different I won't even recognize myself."

PIRATES

THUY TRANH HAD SURVIVED PIRATES and starvation on the South China Sea during her escape from Communist Vietnam in the 1980s, and the habits of survival had not not slackened when she reached Indonesia. She discovered that immigration to America was much faster if a family was involved: churches in America would "adopt" them. So she found an alert Chinese-Vietnamese fellow in the refugee camp and explained the matter to him. He looked her over carefully, thought things over for a day, and agreed that marriage was the smartest course. The marriage was largely a yoking of economic ploughhorses, but overall a success. Love came with the years, two children, and fattening bank accounts.

Thuy's house had garage-sale furniture and, for the first ten years, second-hand kitchen appliances. The decoration was department-store paintings of Italian peasants, bought to fend off the objections of her few American friends who decried the formerly blank walls. Thuy (pronounced *twee*) spent no more than necessary on clothes: functional, baggy, rugged, uncreasable.

She could scarcely understand the expense of restaurants when she could cook meals for a tenth of the price; vacations bored her after a few days and she regretted the time away from her business, but her husband's employer paid for them and the kids had fun. Her husband worked in a a pipe factory 8 to 4, a Chinese takeout restaurant four evenings a week, and a garden center on weekends. Only on their children did they spend lavishly: good clothes, piano lessons, private high schools, Chinese lessons so that the kids could learn to read and write Chinese as well as speak it, for it was rumored that a knowledge of Chinese would be a great plus in their future employment chances.

But Thuy knew that you had to be careful in America; pirates operated here as well. She and her husband had been gypped by the car-insurance company, given bare-minimum service by doctors, taken for a ride by immigration lawyers, and scammed by one of her husband's employers, who had taken out seven percent of his paycheck for years, for IPP: "Oh, that's Integral Insurance Payment, like FICA," his boss had said. "It's only for workers in the restaurant business, but if you get hurt, like you get a grease burn or something, you get paid 152 percent of salary for the time you're out." They had even been scammed by their daughter's college, which had hidden payments from them and then refused to change their financial package. After twenty years in America,

Thuy and her husband had a low opinion of smily American *niceness* that took advantage of their jury-rigged English and scant knowledge of the country. They never made a move without consulting two different lawyers or specialists.

Despite all of this, the family grew richer: her husband was going to start his own Chinese restaurant and probably a messenger service too. Wealth was the measure, simple as a tulip, of happiness.

So she only blamed herself when her flowers-and-plants stand on fashionable Nicollet Avenue in Minneapolis was burgled. Her neighbor, an excitable woman called Latifa, would later screech about the "violation" of her property. (Thuy had to look up the word in her dictionary). But in truth Thuy did not feel this. Looking at the remaining crumbs of glass in the frame, she felt only anger at herself: pirates were everywhere. Just the year before she had turned down an offer of triple-thick safety glass, with free installation.

Foolish, foolish, she told herself in Vietnamese, sweeping up the glass into some wrapping paper — the wasted sheet cost her another 37 cents. *Foolish, foolish. With pirates everywhere.* They had robbed three poinsettas as well, and because Thuy grew everything in her backyard greenhouse, it was sixty dollars of pure profit down the drain: it was a week before Christmas and poinsettas were selling like crazy.

She carried the glass gently to the wastebasket down the street and poured it into the waste basket, and after a careful perusal of the paper decided that she could cut off a dirty six-inch strip and wrap small plants in it. She took apart a rose box and taped it over the broken pane: 86 cents lost. The robbery must have occurred shortly before her Saturday opening time of noon, she reflected, since the remaining plants hadn't suffered from the December cold. *Foolish, foolish — you never learn your lesson about the pirates. You should have bought the security glass. Another fifteen minutes, and you would have lost every single plant.* Thuy had no property insurance: it was an extra expense, and a healthy bank account, she had learned, was a far more reliable insurance.

Then she saw the note.

It was a small Post-It, a little larger than a postage stamp; until then covered by her gloves. The writing was a woman's, the ink green: *Sorry about window. Back 1-2-3.* And a wind-blown smile face; or at least one corner of the slashed-on mouth turned vaguely upwards.

A thief who left a note: unbelievable. "Life in America's just a shocker a day, baby," Latifa always said with a grin.

Thuy re-read. *Sorry about window* — that was clear enough. *Back 1-2-3* she associated with those morning exercise shows she had watched at home in the weeks after giving birth. English for Thuy was a hostile river which could be crossed only upon the stepping stones of vocabulary that she was sure of; her husband's was better. *Back 1-2-3.*

Were they giving exercise advice in exchange for the flowers? A dumb idea, maybe, but so was leaving an apology at a robbery.

Christmas shopping was heavy that day and the rest of the poinsettias sold out fast. Thuy remembered the thieves. *Sixty dollars — a big loss.* The window she could have fixed for free: her cousin Vang, who was a carpenter and the only one of six members her family who had survived the boat voyage and refugee camps with her, could cut a glass and repair the hole. Unmarried, he lived with her family; his workshop was the left side of Thuy's garage. By noon, Thuy was turning away customers asking for poinsettias: "No more poinset's, not in nowhere," she argued. "The orchids good plants and get last more long. Maybe years, you take care." But only twice was she able to divert the customer to another plant. She cursed the thieves and their families back to their greatest of great-grandfathers.

And then the thieves appeared.

It was two-thirty, and the shopping rush had declined for the moment. Thuy was storing money in her hiding place: under the false top of her wrapping table — built for her by her cousin. When she turned around, a young blond woman with a heavy face stood in the doorway; behind her was a middle-aged man in an open coat. Their car was parked, illegally, by the curb, its emergency lights blinking.

"Hi! Are you the proprietor?" squeaked the woman. Feet together, back bowed forward the way Thuy didn't like because it made her feel like a child. The re-settlement people from the Lutheran church had done that, and years later she still resented it.

Thuy didn't know the last word, but she guessed it. "Yah — dis my shop," she said guardedly. These weren't customers. Sales reps, maybe. She placed her hand neutrally in the woman's extended one. Evangelists? No. They dressed too well.

The man squeezed an arm between the door-frame and the woman. "Hi! I'm Jack. This is my assistant, Diane. And you are...."

It took Thuy a moment to realize this was a question. "My name Thuy."

"Did you find our note?" asked the woman. Her mouth turned tragic, her shoulders sagging to one side.

Now Thuy understood. "Oh! Yah! Hey — get my window broken. Got pay. Three plan."

"You're absolutely right, Thuy," said the man. "And we have every intention of making good on that count. Let me explain."

The girl scooted out of his way, and the man filled the doorway, pressing Thuy back against her table. His oiled hair was parted on the side so perfectly he might have been a birth defect. He wore a red tie, and Thuy wondered again — she saw so many of them downtown — if this denoted some kind of class distinction or officialdom. The suit jacket lapel beneath the coat held a crushed white boutonniere; it hung on, upside down.

"Y'see, our company had its Christmas lunch today: seventy-eight hundred dollars of buffet, ambiance pianist, wine waiters and gold ingots for all employees." A laugh. "Believe me: nothing I would wish on my worst enemy."

"He means the organizing it all," said the woman anxiously from the side.

"Ah. Org'nize. Yah — lot wo'k." She wondered why they were explaining this. Perhaps they were going to ask her to forgive the debt, and tension rose within her because she scarcely had the command of English to argue a point successfully.

"This *redefines* the word 'a lot,' Thuy, let me tell you."

"Refine — yah," said Thuy uncertainly.

"And coming on top of the quarterly *and* yearly sales forecasts," said the man.

"I haven't gotten home before ten since *November*!" exclaimed the woman over his shoulder.

"And then we got tapped for the Christmas lunch! The language from HR was crystal clear: do it and do it right."

Thuy had heard Latifa use the term *HR* in regard to her job at the airport, and it was some kind of evil boss. "Yah: HR — bad."

The woman: "That's the thing: our HR has always been pretty stripped-down. Otherwise, they'd've taken care of it."

The man: "Well, you bite the bullet and you do it."

A bullet? The conversation was beginning to alarm Thuy. "Hey — what kind company?"

"We're in securities, Thuy — you know, all kinds of equity, instruments, derivatives, straddles, some currency action."

"You got a office?"

"You're standing right in front of it!" the man laughed. He pointed to the monstrous glass shaft on the other side of the sidewalk.

"Jack, we've got to get moving," said the woman, jumping nervously from one foot to the other. Thuy wondered if she had to go to the bathroom. That was a problem with her stand: she had no bathroom. She was going to tell her to go across the street to the Nigerian restaurant — Jefferson, the head cook, didn't mind — when the man continued.

"Okay, bottom line is, Thuy: we're in the staff meeting room, fifteen minutes to go till the lunch, and we're hauling around the gold ingots to put beside the plates and setting out the plants — one to a table, right? — and it turns out we're *three short!*"

"We got the number of tables wrong!" cried the woman from behind him.

"*Diane* — it's the *caterer* who got the number of tables wrong." To Thuy: "And of course, we didn't have time to condense places of twenty tables back to seventeen." He flapped his hands hopelessly. "And there you are: fifteen minutes to opening, the first employees — with spouses — starting to arrive, and we have three tables without poinsettias. What the hell do you do?"

"I called *two different* downtown florists!" cried the woman, showing Thuy her cell phone. Her shoulders sagged even more, as if she were carrying a buckets of water from the well. "*Nobody* had any left!"

"Yah — get sell lot today. Season."

The woman "And I remembered your shop and we came tearing down here."

"And then you weren't open! How could you *do* this to us, Thuy?" said the man with a grin, throwing his arms wide.

"Open late Sat'day — twelve clock." she pointed to the sign on the side of the stand.

"Right: twelve o'clock — isn't that the baddest of bad luck?"

"Hey, why you not buy othe' plan'? Orchid — last long time." She turned and gestured to the orchids on display. "You take care, ten year. Only need a little — "

"Thuy, Thuy, Thuy," said the man, smiling and shaking his head. "We're talking a 7.6-billion pretax enterprise. Offices in 137 cities worldwide, investments where no man has gone before. They don't pay us to leave three tables without poinsettias. They pay us for tables *with* poinsettias *and* on time. And there's no screaming job description. Like I told Diane, results are results for the janitor just like they are for the CEO."

"You just can't believe what it's like in there," Diane giggled, rolling her eyes in wonder. "I mean, it's like, if you have to stay up all night to get the work out, you just bring your toothbrush to work and do it. You would not *believe* the burnout rate."

"Yah. Bur' out. Bad," Thuy murmured. Latifa used this term often.

"But you see the spot we were in, Thuy?"

"It was awful!" Diane moaned.

"There we were, looking through the window at your beautiful poinsettias. And I say to Diane, 'Diane, we are *here*, and the goal is *there*.'" He shook his head and chuckled. "The answer was more than clear." He raised an arm and jabbed the air with his elbow.

"Yah. You break window, maybe plants freeze. I come, still okay. I hurry make ca'dboa'd. Save plants."

"Gosh, that's right!" said Diane, grabbing one cheek in horror. "Jack! We could have destroyed her whole stock!"

"Well, the point is we didn't," said the man with irritation. "And we're *deeply* sorry, Thuy, about the glass and everything. But Secur — our company — is an honorable firm and we're going to compensate you for your pain and suffering *right now*." He was pulling out his wallet. "No lawsuits, no insurance forms to fill out, no mess, nothing: the way things ought to be. We are going to nip this thing totally in the bud."

The wallet was a sleek, supple membrane of black leather. Thuy saw a colorful rank of credit cards and a wad of bills. The man slipped out the entire group of bills and handed them to Thuy.

"That's 650 dollars in twenties and fifties, fresh out of Petty Cash — and I practically had to pry it out of Dolores Arnold's cold, dead hands."

"Yeah, she guards the Petty Cash box like you're taking it out of her pocket!" the woman cried.

The man smiled. "Are we even?"

The money had a perceptible weight in Thuy's hand. "Even," Thuy muttered uncertainly, for she knew this word as the opposite of "odd."

"Great, Thuy. And that's *with* our thanks." He grabbed her right hand and shook it.

"And we're *really, really sorry* again," added the woman, also shaking her hand. "Thanks *so much*. You've really helped us out of a jam."

In a moment, they had retreated to the car and were gone. Thuy quickly stored the money in the false top of the wrapping table. Six hundred fifty dollars for a broken window and three plants. Not bad. It would pay for the triple-thick safety glass.

She stepped out onto the sidewalk and ran her eyes up the gargantuan glass building: 52 stories, she'd been to the top with her kids once. It troubled her that the people inside worked so much. She'd always thought it was easy, clean work — and if you missed a few days because of illness, they still paid you. But those companies really cracked the whip too: working till ten o'clock every night!

Or sometimes overnight! She had thought that only immigrants did that. The fight for survival, apparently, was far more widespread. To break a window and steal poinsettias! For an office lunch! On a Saturday! That was real desperation: their boss must be even worse than her husband's at the pipe plant.

She went back into her stand and began re-arranging the plants to display them better in the windows. From a drawer she took the business card of the safety-glass man and put it in her pocket; she would have her husband call him later on. You couldn't be too safe, she figured. Pirates were everywhere, and they might not be so foolish the next time.

EXPOSURES

*"I didn't sing [in concert] for 27 years because
of that night ... I was like, 'God, I don't know. What
if I forget the words again?'"*
— Barbra Streisand

I LISTENED TO SARA NOGAL'S LATEST ALBUM — just out in Portugal and sent to me by a colleague at the Lisbon branch — on the way to the restaurant, trying to like it. No good. Yes, the voice was magnificent, but now, in a complete reversal, she was singing pop, not Portuguese *fados* and her own dark, brooding compositions: the mountains, leafy villages, workers cutting cork from the trees, barrels of silently-ripening wine, Coimbra in a winter rain, the cod fisherman who must thread themselves into port through with the rockiest coastline in the world. This album had a Barry Manilow ballad awkwardly translated to Portuguese, a Broadway oldie, and blatant cuts of American Seventies pop. The only vestiges of her first album were two traditional Portuguese folk songs — not bad, but....."

"Sara Nogal has gone glitz," I muttered after each song. "One good album and she goes glitz. Nothing is sacred anymore."

The restaurant was a steak place along the highway with topless waitresses. We met there about every six months: it was quiet and dark, and halfway between our homes in Dayton and Cincinnati; and because the waitresses served you and disappeared until you called for the bill. We were more than just friends and former football teammates; we were each other's biographers. At our dinners we noted the ever-shrinking scope of our athletic potential, analyzed the disillusions and surprises of marriage and parenthood, and reviewed the darkening landscape of politics and the economy.

"So how'd it go with Sara Nogal?" I asked once we'd gotten past the usual bearhugs and ordering of food. "Isn't she great?"

Jay settled back into the booth and took a big gulp of red wine and sighed. "Jesus, Al. Right off the bat. You could have let me get a little tanked first." His round face was smaller, reduced — eroded somehow; I'd already told him that he'd lost weight, and there were no false compliments between us. He'd gone from chunky tackle, which he used to be, to reasonably stocky tight end.

"Is she great?" Jay repeated thickly. "If you mean the voice — you know, the sound — yeah, absolutely. Everything you said: voice that'd launch a thousand ships."

"What's the matter? Didn't she show up?"

He swallowed more wine and watched his fingers huddle around the stem of the glass like sailors around the mast of a sinking ship. "Oh yeah, she showed up all right. Complete washout. We even received a letter of protest from the Portuguese Embassy."

"*What?*"

"Thank god they're foreigners — otherwise we'd be in court covering our ass for years."

I sipped Rioja and waited.. If friendship is a successful coincidence of mutual assumptions, questions are largely superfluous

He dragged his coat across the booth seat and dug in the pocket. "Here's your CD back." He laid it on the table and pushed it away as if it were a turd. "S.o.b.'s been sitting on my dresser looking at me for months."

On the CD cover — her first album — Sara Nogal stood on a high cliff over the sea, hair streaming back in the wind. She had a pretty, angular face, the dark complexion of the Portuguese, thin shoulders — thin everywhere, really, a fragile slip of woman not yet twenty at the time. You marveled that such a trumpeting voice issued from such a small vessel.

I had put Jay on to her. Setting up my company's Lisbon branch the year before, I had come across her music. Her first album had just come out, and her star was starting to shoot. When Jay e-mailed me that he was looking for a young foreign singer for an episode of the hidden-camera gag series he was producing ("Soft stuff: the sponsors make diapers for the elderly."), I put him on to her. Sara Nogal's manager jumped on the chance for American exposure.

"All right," Jay was saying, "so me and the techies move into the high school music room on Saturday morning and get everything set up. I have to sit at the grand piano and sing "Mary Had a Little Lamb" for three hours till the sound specialist gets everything ready. That was the only tough point on the contract, y'know. Miss Nogal's manager — guy named Anastasio — insisted that the sound had to be first-rate. The week before, we'd even paid to get the piano re-tuned — on a Saturday too. High school principal said the tune-up would pay off the favor of using the class."

He drank. "Okay. By seven Saturday night, we had the sound done, the secret cameras and mics in place, a control center set up in the teachers' break room right next door — everything ready. Miss Nogal had arrived a few days before to get over the jet lag. On Sunday, I drive them to the high school for the run-through. I go over the gag again with Miss Nogal, and she loves it."

"What's she like?" It was a casual fan question. I didn't get a casual answer.

"Oh, God. Nobody who should be in show business, Al — I'll tell you that from the start. Or if she is, she ought to be doing some elite stuff, like opera or something. She's" — he thought — "I don't know. Nervous? Is that it? Reedy? Or maybe that's part of it. She reminded me of this gravity-measuring gauge my uncle's company markets. So fragile, if you just *touch* it, it breaks."

I muttered something understanding — and wondered what on earth had happened, both to Sara Nogal and to Jay.

"Listen, Al: Sara Nogal is this sweet kid from a land where they open doors for each other and go to enormous family sit-down lunches on Sunday and afterwards they sing songs and take an evening stroll. She's smily, nervous, takes orders, polite to her elders and to me. Only time she sort of broke the goody-two-shoes mold was when she sat down at the piano to rehearse her song — had to 'meet' the piano, she said. She spoke this kind of half-and-half English."

"Nice voice, huh?" I said.

He looked away at the corner of the table as if speaking of the dead. "Like you said: Mariah's strength and Karen Carpenter's sweetness." He pointed at the CD with a fingernail. "They didn't fiddle a bit with the sound on this thing, I'll tell you that. Couldn't understand a word, but I didn't give a damn."

"What'd she sing?"

Jay turned over the CD and looked at the songs. "The last one: Fado da Quai."

"My favorite. Just her and the piano to finish off the album."

Jay nodded into his wine. "Yeah — fantastic. More spirit in that song than...." He opened his hands, palms up like a beggar. "But don't you see, Al? That's her problem!"

"Her problem?"

"I mean — shit, I don't know. If you want to answer the riddle of the Sphinx, don't ask a t.v. producer." He drained his glass and filled it again. "All right, let's get this over with and then we can talk about falling stock prices or the hapless Bengals — something pleasant." He loosened his shoulders and neck.

"Like I said, on Sunday, Miss Nogal and Anastasio come in, the music teacher Mr. Edwins comes in, we run through the gag. Me and the janitors and a couple techies sit up in the chorus risers and play the part of the varsity choir. Mr. Edwins comes in with Miss Nogal, he introduces her to the class, says she's a new exchange student from Portugal who will be joining the choir, and invites her to make a brief audition — you know, in order to know where to put her? Soprano or alto section or wherever? O.K. Miss Nogal asks if she can accompany herself on piano. He says 'Oh, you play piano?' — hams it up pretty good, that guy — and she sits down and belts one out that supposed to knock the kids right off the risers. Then John Champlain, the emcee, would run in with the *Surprise Surprise* sign, and ha-ha-ha. We were even going to put on some concert footage of her before the gag started — develop audience superiority, right?" A sigh. "But you know what human nature is."

"Well, what's the matter? Didn't she knock them off the risers?"

"Well, yeah, maybe a little at first."

The waitress came with our onion rings for starters; we hardly looked at her.

Jay ate an onion ring and drank some wine. "Okay. So Monday morning dawns. Bright and early at seven, me and all the techies arrive and we turn on the equipment, make a final check, stash ourselves in the teachers' break room. Anastasio arrives with Miss Nogal at eight, so does Mr. Edwins, and they all go straight to the principal's office. A little chitchat, principal gets an autograph. Kids are trickling into the music room, first bell at eight-ten. And me and John Champlain and these four techies are watching the monitors."

Now his gaze floated up to the far wall; it was looking for salvation, or maybe an escape.

"Then we start noticing something funny. The kids are running all over the room. We'd hidden a mic in the piano, and now they're looking inside. Then one of them goes running over to some music stands on the band risers where we'd hidden a camera — looks like a pen, it's nothing. And one of the kids grabs it and shouts, "'Hey! I got one!'"

I nodded. "They'd found out."

"Yup." He sipped. "Yup. They knew. They knew. Someone in the chorus had gotten the word, it spread. We could see them bunching up in groups and whispering about it."

He raised a hand before I could ask. "I don't know, either, Al. Never found out, never will, don't know, don't care. One of the janitors, probably. Maybe Mr. Edwins, maybe his wife — who knows? A kid came by after basketball practice on Saturday to get some books out of his locker. The janitor told him we were filming an educational video, and that seemed to satisfy him. Maybe it didn't."

"So you had to call off your shoot, and that asshole you have for a boss fired you. Hell, Jay, I've got ten thousand in stocks that aren't doing shit for me. Just say the word, and I'll — "

"That's just it, Al: I *didn't* call it off!" He looked down at his fingers again, and I could almost hear the phrase echoing through his mind: *I didn't call it off.*

"Ah."

"Are you kidding? After getting her out there, setting the whole thing up, spending budget on first-class tickets, a hotel suite and eight free-lance techies? This is show business, for Christ's sake, not a courtroom. You do what any good producer would do: you fake it. You bullshit it through. This is *television*. Even on game shows they run through the contestant's reaction a few times, and believe you me, the grand-prize winner has got to bounce off the fucking walls when he wins, and they'll do ten takes till he does. Viewers want *emotion*."

I considered this. "All right, fair enough. So?"

A drink. "Okay. Remember the scene: I'm standing there watching the monitors and crushing a can of Gatorade in one hand. And I think, 'Well, okay, it's not the most honest gag in the world, but we're going to give this unknown from Portugal a leg up here in the U.S.A.' No bullshit, Al. I was thinking of Sara Nogal. Sales galore once the gag comes out. What the hell, I figure. She'll never know the diff. A win-win situation. And I *believe* in win-win, Al. In fact, that's *all* I believe in anymore." He rubbed his hands as if they were cold, though the room was kept quite warm for the bare waitresses.

"So I run into the music room. I walk in and shout, 'EVERYBODY SHUT UP!' — and they do, boy. I tell the wiseguys to put the cameras and the mics *exactly* back where they found them and tell everybody to get their ass up on the risers. The eight-ten bell rings. I've got the time it takes Edwins and Miss Nogal to walk there from the principal's office to put Humpty Dumpty back on the wall. So I talk turkey. I nicely introduce myself and I say, 'All right, *you* know what's going on, and *I* know it. Here's the deal. This woman is going to sing, you all are going to listen and applaud when she finishes. Then the emcee John Champlain runs in — surprise, surprise — we take a few interviews, and we're all set. When we're finished, I take down everybody's name and you all get two free dinners at the best restaurant in town. Deal?'

"And some wiseass pipes up and says, 'Oh sure — you get the dinners wholesale at the restaurant, and they give you a huge discount.'"

"Kind of people that deserve their bad molars," I said.

"No, no, Al, wiseasses I can handle. No problemo. I say, 'Okay, smart guy, your choice: dinner for two, or two hundred in cash. No discounts. Happy?'"

"Two hundred bucks," I said. "That's pretty generous."

Jay grunted a laugh. "It's nothing! There were roughly forty people in the chorus — comes out to eight grand. Chump change. Champlain's per-show *alone* is twenty." A shrug. "Of course, turns out we didn't have to pay it."

"No?"

"Though when the smoke had cleared, a dozen of the little bastards came up to me with their hands out asking for the bucks."

Jay drank. I drank. A last shot before the jump off the cliff.

"All right. So the kids yell 'Hooray!' and I think I've got everything back on track. I run to the break room, check with the techies, run back in and adjust the camera on the music stand, run out. And *just* as I'm closing the door, I see Mr. Edwins and Miss Nogal coming round the corner down the hall. She's dressed in slacks and a black sweater — a little too elegant for high school, but maybe that's what they wear in a Portugal. Great — the foreign touch.

"I look at the monitors; we're already rolling, you know. All the kids are up on the risers, blabbing about how they're going to spend my eight grand. Mr. Edwins and the girl come in, and they fall dead silent. *Uh-oh*, I'm thinking. *Not good — not natural.* But okay, Mr. Edwins goes into his act, and there are a few nervous giggles here and there, but those can be edited out later on. We record digital — you can do anything, you can put in a whole new crowd noise if you need to. They have their little dialogue, Miss Nogal sits down at the piano and tells everyone that she's going to sing a *fado*: 'a typical Portuguese song of lament,' she says. And this gets a few throat-clearings too, but still nothing we can't handle. And now I'm thinking, 'We've got it. Once she gets into the song, that voice'll blow them away whether they're expecting the gag or not.'"

"I imagine it would."

Jay's index finger leapt and stabbed. "Right! Exactly! That's *exactly* it. Isn't that *exactly* what a reasonable, logical person would think? So Sara Nogal starts singing away with that great voice of hers, and I signal John and the mobile cameraman to go out into the hallway with the sign and be ready to run in, and everything's rolling right along. We're getting some great shots of eyes opening like plates, jaws getting rubbed, heads shaking. One little snot up on the left side is laughing — you can't hear him, but you can see his shoulders shaking. Who cares — we have five different cameras on the kids."

Jay's momentum hit a wall. He sighed at the corner of the table and leaned an elbow on the table and pinched the corners of his eyes together with one hand.

"Come on, Jay," I said. I had to say something, anything. "It can't be that bad."

His voice rose a piggish squeak. "Bad I can handle. I wish it *were* bad." He gave a single curt sob into his napkin. "So Miss Nogal, he whispered, "she's singing this gut-wrenching song that would make a rock cry. And I remember thinking how glad I was to give her a leg up. No kidding — I remember thinking that, Al." A swallow. "She gets through the two stanzas and starts the last refrain — you know, very sad, starts on a long high note, right?"

"Yeah, sure. Beautiful song."

"Well, it was a little *too* beautiful, at least for those little fuckers." Another swallow. "The high note was some kind of catalyst. The whole class broke up laughing. Not giggles. I mean belly-slapping, feet-stomping laughter."

Jay's neck writhed; he might have been tied to the stake with the first wisps of fire nipping at his feet. "And Miss Nogal doesn't hear it for a few seconds — concentration, I guess — and then she does...and she stops, looks up....You can imagine."

I could: the "typical Portuguese song of lament" trashed like someone putting his fist through a painting — with the cruel gusto that only kids are capable of.

"She should never, never have gone into show business," Jay was saying when I could focus my attention again. "Those things happen, you know, and you have to have a thick skin."

"I guess." It was the meager breakwater he had erected for himself, and I left it alone.

The light bulbs in the restaurant were reddish, which was supposed to be sexy, but only served to make the place look like an amusement-park horror house. Silently, we finished the onion rings. I slipped the CD into my coat pocket while Jay was fussing with a handkerchief.

"The kids were great about it afterwards. They got up a petition and made a long scroll with an apology on it, and everybody in school — students, staff, everybody — signed it. Forty-five feet long — pretty nice, with drawings and everything. I Fed-Exed it to her in Lisbon. It must have made *some* kind of impression on her. All the school got back, though, was a two-line letter thanking them for the gesture and signed by Anastasio. I thought he could have been a little nicer — at least an auto-graphed pic from Miss Nogal."

I examined my onion ring — crusted batter around the sweet ring — and very nearly laughed at the symbolism. "What did Sara Nogal do when the kids started laughing?"

"Oh, about what you'd imagine — burst out crying, ran out of the room and to the principal's office, where Anastasio was. Dragged him out to the limo I'd ordered for them to go to the airport in. And she must've looked like hell because thirty seconds later, I've got Doctor Berkowitz, the principal, coming down on top of me like a ton of bricks. And I look at him and I say, 'Hey, *I* didn't laugh at anybody. *I* was doing my job. Blame your fucking juniors and seniors here who behaved like two-year olds.' He did, of course, but you know kids. Some of the girls were pretty upset — they're the ones that got up the scroll — but in general everybody just blew it off, changed channels."

The waitress came with our steaks and soundlessly laid them on the table. "Can I get you gentlemen anything else *from the kitchen?*" she asked: from the kitchen, that is, not *from me*. It was easy to see she'd been grabbed before.

When she'd gone, Jay looked at the meat, hands beside the plate. "Well," he said with a short, hopeless laugh. "Let's eat these great steaks, huh?"

We talked of other things, our marriages, our sex lives, the Bengals, our finances. Jay, incidentally, had nearly lost his job, not because of the incident but because he personally gathered up all the video that had been shot, deleted it, and drove to a river bridge and threw the drives into the water. When he got back to Cincinnati, the company director gave him hell because the scene would have been dynamite for their real-life-drama home-video series the company was producing. Jay told him to shove it.

We left at nine, a bottle of Rioja to the better. A clawing February wind raked our necks in the parking lot, and a few snowflakes were whipping past. We had parked our cars side-by-side, and before Jay got into his, he piled his arms on the roof and said, "You know, Al, I told you a lie in there. And I don't want this stuck under my skin till next time we get together."

I waited.

"Look, I didn't FedEx the scroll to Sara Nogal. I took it in person."

"To Lisbon?"

"Cost me twelve hundred bucks and a couple nights of hotel. I told Fran" — his wife — "about everything, and she understood. All the company knew was I was taking a few days off."

I pulled up my coat collar; the wind was merciless and the snowflakes zapped me electrically. Jay seemed not to notice.

"I flew to Lisbon, went to Anastasio's office, told him I wanted to apologize to Miss Nogal for everything and give her the scroll. He looked at a yard or two of it and made some shitty comment about how Americans think that bigger is always better. Wind-up was he wouldn't let me see her. Said she was too busy preparing her next album. She wasn't. The secretary — I kind of knew her from calling her so many times to set up the shoot — she told me she was at some beach resort down south, recovering. She'd come back a wreck.

Trouble sleeping, lots of prescriptions, canceled her schedule."

"Jesus."

Jay looked away down the highway. The cars flung past. "You're right about Lisbon — nice town. Pretty, no junk. Kind of Old-World comfy-innocent. Rickety trams, decent glass of wine for a buck. Women know how to dress too."

I opened the door of my car. "Well, her second album just came out, so she must have gotten over it," I lied.

"Maybe." Jay stared into the dark; guilt hit him openly like waves against a shore; a life of victories and bracing challenges had left him no defenses. "Maybe. She should have gone into opera or something."

We parted. I played Sara Nogal's latest CD again, trying to like it, but no luck. It was awful: a voice singing lyrics, its soul protected by a carapace of mainstream pop.